Johnny Blue and the Righteous Spin

John Allen Machado

This is a work of fiction. Names, characters, places, and incidents either are the
product of the author's imagination or are used fictitiously, and any resemblance
to actual persons—living or dead—businesses, companies, events, or locales is
entirely coincidental.

For Joan

PART I

"The only way to make sense of change is to plunge into it, move with it, and join the dance."
–Alan Watts

One

Johnny Blue was one cool customer. But he wasn't always that way. Somehow, someway, he developed into a walking, breathing calmness with a keen awareness for the absurd. Yet even he couldn't escape being naked and on display and vulnerable to the overabundance of humanity's viscous judgments.

Two-thirds through his life, at thirty-four, a slight yet powerful change in thought process occurred, what some business and spiritual books refer to as a paradigm shift. Call it what you want—wisdom, experience, common sense, or simply stripped-down know-how and figuring shit out. Fact be known, Johnny Blue spent too many years ignoring everything outside his pleasure perimeter. Thus, he was oblivious to his immediate and extended surroundings if there was nothing in it for him: me first, me last, me in-between.

Then, for some odd reason, that self-absorbed trend was altered as he stumbled into a newfound awareness opening his eyes to the apparent, the obvious, and the selfishness of it all. He was literally granted a second chance, a chance at soul repair.

The new Johnny Blue could sniff out the slightest contradiction in a New York minute, as well as the repeated ridiculousness being spewed by the many. Opposite that, he also experienced an undeniable genuineness and its range of clarity blew his mind: the rare few lacking hidden agendas, with their anxieties and insecurities in check. Those brave listeners and doers of good who aren't seeking reward or payout or meritless attention—refusing to push for fictional narrative to win out, refusing to sway under false pretenses. Johnny Blue didn't just reach out and grasp this fresh angle of thinking; but instead, readily accepted its insertion as if mainlining pure truth into an open vein.

Johnny Blue was born and raised smack-dab in the geographical middle of middleclass America. Everything surrounding his life was slanted in the direction of middle this or middle that.

1. He was a middle child.

2. His mother was a career middle school teacher.

And 3, 4 & 5. His father worked in mid-level management for an insurance company and played center for a local recreational hockey club that went by the name of the Middle-Aged Blades.

The Blue clan was the epitome of a family portrait oozing suburbia. Johnny Blue grew up choking on the thought that everything was as it should be. Conflicted, he understood clearly his early lot in life—having parents, a sister and brother, friends, a nice home, and daily food on the table, what the average suburbanite thought to be normal.

He held nothing against his folks or siblings for the way they lived their lives, appearing as if all was well and orderly. But in the extreme depths of his being, Johnny Blue inherently knew he never wanted that form of skewed stability. For he dwelled in contrasting spectrums, by far preferring chaos and high-intensity emotion. And if not in a state of disarray, then he was gravely bored, with absolutely no attention span whatsoever for the mundane.

While growing up, Johnny Blue's best friend and running mate was a quiet, wiry kid who loved getting into mischief with Johnny as much as Johnny enjoyed the same with him. Rob Zamora played Foggy Nelson to Johnny's Matt Murdock. Calm and demure on the outside, Rob was more than game to whatever he and Johnny decided to leap into, as if being together brought out a certain level of rambunctiousness that would have remained dormant had their paths not crossed.

What they both had in common—besides their daring nature—was an inherent decency. They never played roughshod bully to anyone's cowering victim and were always willing to fess up to shenanigans-gone-wrong when to do so needed to be done. Their relationship stayed strong and consistent until early adulthood when Rob went off and joined the Marine Corps while Johnny, eyeing the prize of a future career in sales, strode into college fully determined to make something of his life. But stay in touch they would, sporadically so, yet, friends for life and all that until the end.

Johnny's mom and dad, Faye and Dale, were diligent parents in a make-believe storybook kind of way. As adult role models treading water through the crosscurrents of parenthood, they attempted to be consistent, attempted to be who they thought they were supposed to be and didn't attempt to be anything other than that, to include who they really were. They enjoyed their journey from being high school sweethearts to then attending the same university before finally getting married soon after college graduation. And once they began their respective careers, they'd stay put until eventual retirement.

The biggest reward for Faye and Dale was in fact parenthood, especially when providing timely, sound advice to a child in want. All three children had completely different personalities, with Johnny being strong willed and gregarious when out and about, yet a quiet, introspective loner when in the confines of domestic swaddle. While butchering a quote from Thoreau, they sometimes referred to their middle child as "someone who kept pace to the beat of an odd bass." But they openly accepted all three as they were, giving them plenty of room to figure things out—with the lengthiest section of rope freely extended to Johnny Blue.

Johnny's relationship with his siblings was that of an ongoing, informal observation. For the most part, he kept them at a distance— older sister, younger brother—spending very little time with either one. When in their company, he observed their individual traits and how they went about their lives as if watching monkeys traipse around a protected zoo enclosure. Actual communication with either one only took place when necessary, with concise verbal interchange being the utmost priority.

Maria, who would become a nurse, and Nathan, an accountant, thought their brother to be a bit off if truth be known. But over time they found him to be a standup guy despite his peculiar nature. Neither one, nor anyone else for that matter, could have accurately predicted Johnny Blue's future. Their honest reaction to his eventual fate was that of total astonishment, like when an underdog team wins a championship that faithful fan never saw coming.

Two

She was only the second person I'd ever met who I wanted to make happy. Everyday. All the time. Her happiness made me happy. And it was easy to pull off because she was chill as chill could be, what the average non-PC-Paul calls "a low maintenance chick."

She loved art, particularly paintings. That's what she told me the first night we met, adding that it was especially important that art, any art, be original art. She was not a big fan of prints or copies, saying that most Americans were caught up in the deception of replicas, reproductions. Hoodwinked they were by overpriced duplicates. Copies of copies. Unoriginal.

I bought her quite a few pieces of art—all original save one—ranging from good, to not so good, to outstanding. I was astonished by how reasonably priced some topnotch, yet obscure artist's paintings were, cheaper than a lot of popular, below average prints. I found an artist from Grenada who painted little masterpieces. Beautiful paintings: oils, mosaic imagery, abstract. Optic excellence. Those paintings made her happy, made her smile, ponder. Ever the observer.

Man, I loved her. It's weird, though, because I always felt lost without her. I am lost without her.

I met her after I retired—retired on the cusp of forty after spending twenty-one years in the Marine Corps. Then nine wonderful years of marriage with her. Married three months to the day after our initial encounter.

Then she got sick. My Canadian sweetheart fell ill. I made her happy up until the very end, up to her final request. I acquiesced. She thanked me with her eyes.

I miss her so much that it hurts beyond the definition of hurt. Hurts to take a breath, to think, to exist. What a wonderful human being she was. I was lucky to have met her, let alone love her and be loved by her.

Now what?

Three

Johnny Blue woke up hungover and soon realized he was lying in his own sheet-soaked urine. He was on top of the world, his oyster, and certainly his piss because he woke up alone.

On the professional side of the ledger, Mr. Blue was the top dog of the number one sales team for the number one maker of carbonated sugar water. To be factual: carbonated corn syrup water, with corn syrup being the cheaper sweetener. Cheaper won out, again.

And when not playing the role of successful businessman, Johnny thought himself to be a regular guy who just happened to have a drinking problem and a drug problem (both legal and not) and a sex problem and a food problem. Basically, he had a massive consumption problem in the land of mass consumption. So, in essence, he fit right the fuck in.

As he got out of bed, he ran a hand through his hair and began laughing, then cackling, then howling; like a crazy man, as he adjusted his balls with the other hand. He survived another cocaine-alcohol-pharmacology induced bender. Hell yeah. Indestructible motherfuckers.

He stripped the bed of its linen and headed for the utility room—damp sheets rolled up in a ball. As he passed through the living room he caught sight and sound of a young woman snorting a foot-long rail of cocaine. She was naked except for a pair of black shiny pumps and had that sexy, 1980s Pat Benatar look about her: *Love is a battlefield.*

He stopped and stared. She finished the line then looked his way, rubbing her nose and blinking wildly, attempting to alleviate the fresh, harsh burn.

"You're up," she said.

"I am," he retorted.

"Where're you taking those sheets?" she asked.

"To the laundry room," he replied, the scent of stale piss piercing his nostrils. He decided to breathe through his mouth.

"We didn't fuck in your bed," she stated as a matter of fact.

"Yeah, I know," he lied, as he continued toward the laundry room.

He had absolutely no clue as to who she was, nor did he remember any sexual escapades from the previous evening. Evidently coke and alcohol were involved. And a woman. What was her name? Not the first time forgetting what happened the night before. He sensed details right there at memory's edge. Too much effort, though. Fuck it.

He stuffed the sheets in the washing machine, added laundry detergent, and set the controls at a heavy clean cycle. Returning to the front room, he stopped, looked her way, and suddenly realized that he, too, was naked. She looked at his stuff and he looked at hers. They both became aroused and, well, one thing led to another.

Ninety minutes later—both freshly showered and dressed—he held the front door open for her; a haphazard attempt at chivalry, at manners. Thumbing away at her phone, she stepped out on the stoop while squinting at the midday brightness. Once done texting, she turned to him, and said, "Since you probably don't remember, my name is Shari. I work for an escort service and you paid three thousand dollars for me to spend the night last night. And, you were pretty wasted by the time I got here. But don't worry, you were still able to perform, with the help of a little blue pill of course."

All Johnny Blue could muster was an, "Oh," and "of course."

She added, "I would have normally charged you extra for the session this morning, but I was really horny and figured we were even-steven since I finished off all your coke."

"How much blow did I have?" Johnny asked.

"Right around two eight balls," she replied. Adding, "Give or take."

"Holy shit," he stated. Then asked, "Are you going to be all right?"

"I'm fine. In fact, I'm really, really fine," she said, as she smiled and winked and walked away, her Uber driver right on time.

'Goodbye forever, Shari,' he thought, after walking back inside the condo and pressing his forehead against the cool, smooth surface of the closed front door.

Four

When stripped of its layers of camouflage, what does an average life really look like?

Dale was nervous as hell, guilt-ridden, and about to admit to his wife that he'd been having an affair; a year-old affair with a woman at work—a younger woman. A woman who did certain sexual things that he was too embarrassed to ask his wife to do. In his mind, his prudish spouse wouldn't even consider doing those sorts of things. Angst and shame aside, he was going to miss those naughty encounters.

Truth be told, Faye couldn't have cared less. She would rather some other woman fuck Dale than her, dreading the infrequent sex she felt obligated to have with him as it was—two to three times a year, max. At least now she could act pissed off, disappointed, feelings hurt: "How could you do this to me, to our family?" Faye would let him grovel, but she'd eventually take him back, crawling, begging, and then manipulate the shit out him if he strayed off course. Her course. A pathetic status quo of sorts for the empty nesters.

However, Faye would not admit her affair to Dale, also with a fellow employee and also with a woman. Her boss. The principal at the school where she taught pre-algebra. Her lover was married as well. To a man. And they would both stay married for the time being while continuing their affair. Have their cake and eat it too.

Hypocrisy? Yes. Admittedly so.

But they understood the professional benefits of their continued legal unions, as well as the sexual comforts of a wanted lover. And if they each had to take one for the team a couple times a year, then so be it. It was all about continuing the façade of normalcy in their family lives.

These women were focused, keeping their eyes on the prize. Patience. Timing. A marathon, not a sprint.

Maria surprised the entire family when she left the Midwest and moved to Northern California with someone fifteen years her senior. They were even more surprised after learning that the couple had stopped along the way in San Francisco to get married before heading up to Humboldt County to settle down.

Surprise number three was hurled their way when Maria let them know that she was pregnant with twin girls. And just when everyone thought they were fresh out of surprises, Maria announced that she and her new husband, Dr. Bob, were going to work at the local hospital and also grow weed (as in cannabis) in their big old barn on their newly purchased five acres of Humboldt County real estate. Holy Duke! And that's what Maria and Dr. Bob did, exactly what they said they were going to do.

Nathan looked and acted the part of a starched business executive, a CFO for a private equity firm specializing in money management and corporate takeovers. He had arrived, thinking he was special because his professional title began with a capital "C."

To a blind fault, though, Nathan was not a people person, remaining friendless since childhood and proud of that fact. The social topper, he did not give a rat's ass about anybody but himself. A bit of a cheese-dick, really. So to easily distance himself from most folks, he would either ignore them or, if forced into conversation, purposely wear them down by droning on and on in the most up to date version of copycat corporate-speak—annoyingly laying down predictable buzz words as if coming up with them all on his own.

There were, however, a few things he did cherish, like long periods of silence and the logic of integers. Yes, numbers. Nathan was paid extremely well to produce a prearranged numerical order that favored his employer, a favoring that often bordered on unethical and at times overlapped into illegal. Despite the enjoyable characteristics of his J-O-B, there was one corrosive irritant that scratched away at a tender scab—having to make sense of his numerical deeds to those not as smart as he. In his mind this was a waste of time, what he referred to as "a dumbing down for the clowns."

Condescension aside, Nathan was a bean counter through and through. And he could certainly count those beans, move them around and force balance a spreadsheet or two or fifty. And if you selected what you thought to be the correct shell in the shell game of corporate finance, the very shell you were convinced those beans lie under, you would become unpleasantly surprised after lifting the shell tinged with hope only to find that the beans went missing.

Poof. Nada. All gone.

Because, you see, Nathan was a thief. A white-collar thief who knew what he was doing. Better yet, he knew how not to get caught and how not to leave a detectable trail. He worked hard at his thievery, making the extra effort at being a staunch, disciplined criminal, as in the ones who effectively avoid detection, the law, and incarceration.

Nathan was married to a woman who liked the finer things in life, a woman content with letting her husband bring home the bacon to pay for those finer things. And as long as she was provided a luxurious lifestyle—to include a country club membership, a competent housekeeper and cook, and an only child enrolled in private school—then nothing else really mattered.

Nathan worked long, well-planned hours six days a week, with a portion of those hours dedicated to pilfering funds and covering up loose ends tied to illicit activities. It was critical that he be the first at work each morning and the last to leave at night. This gave him plenty of uninterrupted private time to think and scheme while also presenting the image of a dedicated executive.

And all he wanted in return was a well-kept quiet home, a neat glass of expensive Scotch whisky on Saturday nights, and indelicate Sunday morning sexual encounters before getting ready for church. Oh yeah, and a shitload of money stashed in multiple offshore bank accounts.

Five

It wasn't a dream or joyful fantasy. It was a reality, an actual memory from a distant time. And it usually resurfaced when he was in a solid state of mind, a mindset flowing in warmth for humanity.

He remembered it like it was yesterday and not seventeen years prior, a life altering moment for sure. The twins were now in their twenties. Back then, six or seven, tops. He loved them as if they were his own. They showed him a love he had never experienced and wasn't so sure existed outside of make-believe.

He'd flown out to California to see his sister, meet her husband and kids. The little girls were excited as all get-out to meet their Uncle Blue. That's what they called him, not Uncle Johnny but Uncle Blue. A child's rationale that stuck.

When he got out of the rental car they came running from the house, exhilaration peaking as they darted off the front porch, each in a sundress, neither wearing shoes. Angela took his right hand and Isabella his left.

They steered him back to the porch for introductions with their mom and dad. Maria began laughing, and said, "Yeah I know, he's my brother." The girls thought this to be the funniest thing they'd heard in quite some time and joined in the laughter. Finally, they all went inside to eat a late lunch, sitting on benches at a narrow table in the corner of a sunlit kitchen. Johnny faced Maria and Dr. Bob; all the while bookended by curious nieces spying his every move.

After lunch, the girls implored Uncle Blue to take them for a walk in the woods. Maria and Dr. Bob attempted to intervene, attempted to save him. "Happy to accompany the little ladies on an adventure through the forest," Johnny finally said. The girls erupted in cheerful glee. Victorious. "However," he told the twins, "I need to change into more comfortable shoes." They both giggled, before simultaneously asking, "Why would you wear shoes?" So instead, he changed into shorts and a T-shirt and off they went.

The nearby forest was part of Maria and Dr. Bob's property, with additional acreage extending into county- or federally-owned land depending on direction. From small clearing to dense foliage, their property was surrounded by forest on all four sides, a rectangular speck in the middle of lush, thick landscape.

It had to have been a combination of the girls and nature, their unwavering love plus the trees and coastal fog. That's what stood out in his mind. That's what would always stand out in his mind when he went back to that place: earthy smells, salt-splashed air, love, tranquility.

It was like the twins and the trees and the fog were communicating without words. And he was one hundred percent sober. Very unusual at that point in his life. The turning point. A psychedelic experience sans drugs. If that's possible. It was, because from that day forward sober was what he would be.

They meandered for a good half hour deep into the woods, at last standing before an ancient, majestic redwood. The enormity and height of this erect sentinel was visually overwhelming, stunning. Johnny Blue had never seen such a tree, at least not in person. Knowing that he was in the presence of royalty, he hesitantly reached out and touched it, his hand slowly tracing downward, ever respectful. Its trunk's bark was deeply etched; over-pronounced braille emanating a story for those willing to listen.

Together they sat on the padded forest floor facing the tree, a twin at each side. The fog moved in—much, much thicker—encasing them in a misty-white blanket. Johnny Blue was suddenly overcome by an unexplained deep emotional love and began to weep, as did the twins. All at once they looked up at the giant redwood, its trunk expanding in then out, breathing, shuttering at times, as they all wept in unison.

An understanding. Everyone. Everything. Connected.

Then sleep.

Then, wide awake, fully rested, and returning to the house.

Six

Rob Zamora was a trained sniper. That was his job, what the Marine's had taught him to do. Fine-tuned, polished skills. Eventually a teacher of snipers. Eventually a teacher of teachers who taught snipers.

What he took most pride in—besides taking the critical shot and closing the deal, literally—was organization and preparation. He could not preach those two disciplines enough, to whoever would listen, to include himself. But one still had to conceptually buy in to this killing religion, no half-assed reasoning, and no talking something up just to sound good. You either lived it or you did not. And your biggest enemy was in fact you, your mental game, and your ability to control your ego, the nemesis that could hinder your own survival.

As the beneficiary of a country involved in multiple wars, he was tried-and-battle-tested when everything went to shit, with a high-level emphasis on his two best friends: organized and prepared, especially when chaos reared its ugly head, to which it often did, even during a well plotted skirmish. In his experience, a plan going exactly as planned was rarely the case. It was an anomaly at best.

And one of the worst things that could happen, he often preached, was to pull off a kill when going about your business on cruise control—somewhat prepared, somewhat organized—and to then think you were above executing the basic elements of the craft and that you'd always come out on top: "I'm the best no matter what I do." That damned ego when it leaned on conceit. The killer and savoir of men in combat, a contradiction in terms teeter-tottering on truth and untruth.

What, then, eventually happened to Rob? Simple. He gave up. Not quite completely, but, without a doubt, on the verge of doing so. Mr. Organization and Mr. Preparation no longer visited. He hadn't showered or shaved in way too long and his house reeked of human stench mixed with more than a hint of ripe garbage. Food-splattered dishes lay wherever, soiled laundry strewn about, yardwork and house repair abandoned. That about summed things up.

Rob Zamora had turned into something he would have scorned in what now seemed like a life lived long ago. But he just didn't care anymore, even though at his core he knew for certain she would not have approved. However, she'd been gone a while and he was committed to not giving a shit. And a job well done at that.

Then the phone rang. He looked at it. Decisions?

What bothered Rob the most, more than anything, especially toward the latter stages of his military career, the last five years or so, was that he started to question his career choice: sniper. He no longer thought it to be intertwined with a noble cause, regardless of the rationalizations he'd spewed repeatedly to his students, to his peers, and, inwardly, to himself.

In all honesty, he thought it to be a cowardly profession; a passive-aggressive job where the receiver of bad news gets blindsided by a launched projectile that rips through skin and bone, tearing apart vital organs before exiting the other side without saying hello or goodbye.

He had concluded that there were worse passive-aggressive gigs, like the ones held by the military and political elite. The executive level types. The decision makers. Those responsible for ordering the deaths of thousands of men, women, and children—some enemies, some not—and who do so from the safe confines of modern day war rooms where the aftereffects aren't truly felt, irrespective of the post killing speeches riddled with well-acted, practiced emotions. It's as if sociopath and leader are supposed to be one and the same.

So when he met his future wife, he saw for the first time a comfort and love and understanding tied to human decency. And when she died, he lost that; that which he did not naturally possess. Oh, the horror of dealing with oneself and being alone.

And then the phone rang, again.

Seven

With over a decade of sobriety under his belt, Johnny Blue was once again fed up with life's direction and it had nothing to do with drugs or alcohol or a life altering moment in a forest in Northern California. This time around he'd come to the long, thought-out conclusion that he was tired of jumping through capitalism's manipulative hoop, tired of calculating the achievement equation, and tired of feeling like a five-pound turd in a two-pound sock—smothered and reeking of unimportant shit. He was seeking solutions to a pending madness formed by habitual nothingness. Like the growing few, he was seeking life's purpose and not societal normalcy.

Sobriety wasn't enough anymore. He certainly wanted to stay sober but readily craved change, a change that he could not wholly visualize or wrap his head around. He sensed its lingering presence—whatever it was—knocking on a tiny mental door. And he wanted to uncover this unknown mystery more than he wanted anything else. For him, change paralleled sobriety.

Johnny Blue was in San Francisco, on vacation, walking the streets and taking in the energy of the city. Craving coffee, he ducked into a coffeehouse called The Mad Azorean. Who could resist that name? Right away he sensed a bohemian vibe with an eclectic array of artsy tattoos and interestingly placed body piercings displayed on both the patrons and the employees, making it difficult to distinguish between the two.

After ordering a cappuccino, he looked up into architectural wonderment, eyeing lofty open ceilings retrofitted in hefty slabs of rustic wood and red iron steel. Straightforward, beautiful craftsmanship on display to safely—more like hopefully—ride out high magnitude earthquakes. Order up, he made his way over to a secluded table in the far reaches of the dark lit coffeehouse.

As he sipped his cap, he saw a magazine lying on a nearby table. He reached out and retrieved it, wanting to hang out in the offbeat coffeeshop and get in a little reading. Like a lot of major cities, this homegrown periodical was titled with the city's name followed by the word "Magazine." Far from original, but maybe there was something worth perusing inside the month-old mag.

After breezing by seductive ads pushing a wide range of useless products, he came across what seemed like an interesting article, a feature piece on eco-terrorism covering a relatively recent event in California's central valley where a cattle ranch firebombed by militants hell-bent on protecting defenseless animals from certain death. Johnny Blue thought it odd that he hadn't once heard or read anything from the establishment media referencing this "act of terrorism" as described by the city writer and a representative of the FBI.

After giving the article a thorough read, he felt different—enlightened—in a profound way. But barely a moment passed when the pendulum of feelings swung opposite, causing him to feel utterly stupid and naive, blind and ostrich-like. Suddenly Johnny Blue was dead-set-ready on pulling his head out of the sand. He'd finally received that mental nudge; a shift in thinking he'd been seeking.

With new information pinging in his memory banks, Johnny politely hustled up a pen from a young lady sporting a pink flamingo neck tattoo and an identically colored Mohawk. Getting right to it, he furiously scribbled key takeaways on a brown paper napkin:

1. There is an organization that has existed for some time called the "Liberation of Animals Foundation," or the LOAF for short.

2. The LOAF was formed in Europe in the 1970s.

3. It was founded by a select, trusted group of activists who eventually grew the organization into a worldwide cause.

4. There are no leaders or hierarchy whatsoever within this organization.

5. If you believe in the rights of animals, are a true vegetarian or vegan, and want to fight back against the people who murder and experiment on animals in the cruelest of ways,

then you can oppose these social monsters any which way you deem prudent or non-prudent (i.e., rescue/steal live mink from sure slaughter on Joe Bob's farm in Northern Wisconsin before releasing the little critters back into the wild, or firebomb an industrial cattle ranch and cause millions of dollars in damage). That and the willingness to be a part of the LOAF solidifies membership.

6. And if you are stealth and wise and anonymous, you can go about your freedom fighter/terrorist ways (depending on who is doing the labeling/judging) and hopefully avoid arrest, incarceration, and possibly death.

Hurriedly, Johnny Blue tossed the monthly publication on a deserted table, walked up to the counter and ordered a large cup of coffee to go. With coffee in hand, he headed for his hotel room to conduct needed research on those individuals trudging through society's hidden background who dedicate their lives in retaliation against authoritative bodies dishing out absurd cruelty to the unfortunate, the unlucky, and the preselected unknowing.

As he sat in his hotel room gazing out a window, with the glorious orange bridge appearing small in the distant background, Johnny Blue came to a basic self-conclusion that he quickly keyed into an electronic document:

Think for yourself and act accordingly.

Adding:

Partake in extensive research first.

Not since sitting in a forest in Northern California—in the presence of two little girls and a giant redwood—had he felt so alive.

Eight

With a custom skateboard set beneath skilled nimble feet and a high-grade videocam attached to a Brainsaver helmet, Shakes Montoya rolled down the crowded sidewalk at a decent clip. Darting in and out of the swarm, he occasionally startled on foot commuters immersed in handheld devices—unprepared for city surprises as a skater rips by within mere inches.

With his destination fast approaching, Shakes slowed ever so slightly before power sliding to a complete stop and popping the Maplewood board up into an open hand. He smoothly transitioned from platform to pavement, unzipping his hoodie as he glided inside The Mad Azorean.

After ordering his usual large cup o' Joe with two add shots of espresso, Shakes parked himself on a barstool facing an elongated tabletop that fronted a like-length plate-glass window; in all, thirty feet of voyeur's row. He slowly sipped his ultra-caffeinated beverage, keenly observing the antlike hustle and pace of the city while simultaneously ignoring the goings-on inside the coffeeshop.

Visually plucked from the moving masses, he spotted a familiar face crossing the street and heading for the coffeehouse entrance. Not familiar like he knew the guy, but familiar as in I've seen this dude before. Suddenly it registered that he'd caught sight of this particular gentleman the day prior—at the coffeeshop—sitting in a distant corner and reading some sort of periodical. This unknown man didn't have a touristy way about him, nor the slightest hint of local flavor, either.

Intrigued, Shakes eyed the man as he entered the shop and made a beeline for the "Place Order Here" sign. Then he thought, 'Why am I interested in this guy, this older dude?' Shakes couldn't muster an answer to that question. Regardless of reason why, there was a magnetic force pulling him toward finding out more about this mysterious character. Weird stuff.

After getting a cup of coffee, Johnny Blue headed over to an empty table and took a seat on a worn wooden chair. Uncertainty abound, Shake's stood up and approached the older man, an approach that was much too quick, aggressive, and space invading. Sometimes angst trumps the best of intentions, and that is exactly what happened to Shakes as he found himself staring down at Johnny Blue while standing way too close in what turned into an awkward stranger meets stranger situation.

Johnny Blue handled it well, calmly looking up, leaning back a touch, and saying, "Hi, how're you doing." Shakes took a step back, and said, "Good. You?"

Johnny Blue: Can I help you with something?

Shakes: Yeah. Kind of. (Big breath.) What are you doing here? I don't mean here in this coffeeshop, but here, as in this city. You're not from here and you're definitely not a touristy tourist, if that makes any sense. I know it's none of my business, but I've seen you a couple of times in a couple of days and you seem to be up to something; or, like, maybe you've figured something out. I could be completely wrong, one hundred percent off in my thought process, and way off in my interpretation that what I think and what I see are connected. If you want me to fuck off, I get it. But for some reason I wanted to talk with you, and I'm confused as to why that is.

Johnny, not exactly the trusting type, surveyed Shakes from head to toe as he thought about the very first time he'd ridden a skateboard way back when—an unsuccessful experience that led to an emergency room visit with a broken wrist braced delicately against his body. Done reflecting, he again looked up at Shakes, this time grinning, and said, "Pull up a seat, son."

Shakes: Thanks (taking a seat diagonal to Johnny Blue and placing his board on the floor between both feet).

Johnny Blue: You're an observant young man, and, so far, accurate in your perception of me.

Nine

Blue and Shakes essentially had a two-part conversation. The initial dialogue was dominated by the older man and it went like this:

"You're right in that I'm not from here and I don't approach this city like a tourist. My approach is aligned with that of a future resident. And I didn't come to that conclusion until yesterday while sitting right here in this coffeeshop reading an article in a magazine. An article drenched in clarity that opened my eyes to the absurdity of things, opened my eyes to much more than just the subject matter.

"It's the second time in my life where I figured out what to do next in terms of purpose and direction. No confusion. Zero trepidation. Clear as clear can be.

"Let me give you a quick rundown on me, on some things that are currently on my mind, and then, if you want, you can tell me a little bit about yourself."

Shakes nodded, nonverbally nudging Blue onward.

"I'm from the Midwest, a stone's throw from Omaha. I grew up in a typical middleclass family that if viewed from the outside in appeared to be a highly functional happy clan. We were not. And, honestly, I'm not so sure that that exists. But instead of boring you with personal stories, I'd rather discuss the underbelly of family and society and the correlation that exists between the two.

"Because, you see, with families—with most human dynamics—what predominantly exists is spin. Also, agendas. Everywhere. But a different more hidden agenda with those who've been dealt the grand hand of socioeconomic luck, or, by greater chance, hit the socioeconomic lottery. Simply put, born right place right time right family right country. Pure DNA luck, where the people I'm talking about were either born into a comfortable financial environment; or it was handed down to them (greedy vermin salivating and prematurely counting each dollar while waiting for the holders of older money to die); or they hitched their proverbial wagon to the right money horse; or a combination of all—or a portion of—the things I just mentioned.

"I'm not saying there aren't any self-made folks out there. There are. They just happen to be anomalies. Rare. Not the norm—truly exceptions to the rule and who carry themselves much differently than their obverse leaning contemporaries.

"And do you know what similar traits these lucky people possess? Entitlement, greed, and the fear of losing what they think they deserve; and a certain bitterness and fear toward those who have little or nothing. They fear poverty as if it's a disease. To them it's the boogieman, with the grotesque monster chasing after their stuff, their horded cash, because they could've never earned that money on their own.

"The poor are looked at and treated as if they are of lesser value. And, unfortunately, that has become okay in our society even though it is not okay. Indifference wins out. Capitalistic paranoia wins out. And strident hypocrisy won't allow the admission of truth, because truth and spin can never be aligned. You know, the whole oil and water thing. The only alignment with truth is impeccable truth. And that, my friend, can be a scary road to venture down.

"Poverty is not tied to a cozy existence. Let's face it, poverty kills. It's different in every which way, even when compared to a lower middleclass lifestyle—let alone an affluent one. It's quite clear to me that there is little to no fluff within the world of poverty, with much higher stress factors amongst poor children simply to survive. And sometimes that leads to suicide.

"But for unrelated reasons, the children of parents with money—the so-called well-to-do and entitled—must live with their children killing themselves at a certain rate as well. I'm guessing that these children feel the pressure to compete in their parent's apathetic, capitalistic world, with added strains related to "keeping up with the Joneses" causing depression, eating disorders, drug and alcohol addiction, self-mutilation, and, you name the malady.

"Do entitled children like what they see in their parents? I doubt it, having to listen to repeated, overly spun life stories and trite social media posts about a subpar existence lacking any real struggle. Not a merit-based existence, but a con-based existence directly connected to money manipulation. Do they fear becoming just like their parents? I'm thinking yes, not wanting banal duplication of yet another generation. And that brutal piece of information is pretty apparent to me. Does any of this make sense?"

Quietly paying attention, Shakes said, "Yeah, it does."

"Sorry for digressing. When growing up I did what I thought I was supposed to do even though I resented it, regretted it. The societal norm is suffocating. Always has been, always will be. I followed the predictable middleclass course, stepping into the college thing and then the work thing. I settled for a life I didn't want. And along the way I chose a self-destructive path fueled by self-destructive tendencies.

"But my biggest sin, my biggest regret, has been apathy. I'm fed up with doing those things that just don't matter, don't matter at all. Like the addiction to juggling busy.

"I'm done with that. No more spin. Just truth. I've been searching for something and yesterday I found it.

"It clobbered me right in the face. Batman style. Pow!"

Ten

Neither man spoke—one done talking while the other mulled over options. Then, and very much out of character, Shakes opened up to a perfect stranger and let flow a tale concerning his life story. Something he'd never done before, with anybody.

He'd certainly thought about his life; more importantly, the difficulties surrounding his life, but had kept that shit to himself. Why share? Nobody cares, and fuck being a "Woe is me!" type guy. Now Shakes was about to share some personal stuff with a newly met dude in a coffeeshop in San Francisco, and he was perfectly content with that.

There are a limited number of people you can trust in the short span of a lifetime. The few and far between. But they exist.

And they would never force-feed delusion. Dreadful folks attached to flimsy, one-sided rhetoric will be the first to sway falsely—so-called friends, acquaintances, relatives, whomever—stating bullshit like, "I've always been there for you," even though there's no way to prove such a lame statement. When confronted with hideous trolls hiding beneath dirt-caked bridges, be wary of distorted babble bent in an advantageous direction—theirs, not yours.

The ones that can be trusted have no hidden agendas. Just trustworthy souls with a solid self-worth. Mensch-like. Shakes found that in Johnny Blue, as his story unfolded.

Shakes was born and raised in San Francisco, birthed by a seventeen-year-old with a bipolar disorder. The severity or degree of this medical diagnosis varied greatly depending on the mental health professionals Shakes' mom, Katie, was dealing with at any given time. To top things off, she also self-medicated with quite an assortment of street drugs and alcohol which usually made matters worse.

But most important, she loved Shakes despite her issues and addictions and tried her ass off at being a decent mother. The sad truth was that Katie had to walk away from her child at frequent, temporary intervals until a better mental place surfaced helping her cope with life, helping her fight off personal demons. And even though these temporary intervals were necessary, they brought about additional guilt and misery.

The first ten years of Shakes' life were spent with his mother and her parents—his grandparents. Then grandpa John passed away and grandma Irma ended up in a home, slowly losing a four-year battle to Alzheimer's.

Katie lost the family home when Shakes was fourteen. With her, material loss was inevitable because of the leeches in society who suck blood from the vulnerable. Shakes was eventually passed off to relatives who acted as if they'd taken him in out of the kindness of their hearts; not the case, not even close.

Ulterior motives were involved, as Katie was coerced into handing over whatever extra money she could scrape together to ease the burden of Shakes, a burden that included less than eighty square feet of space, limited food, and the constant vibe of annoyance. For money ruins intent, especially stained money not earned but garnered through falsehoods and other people's efforts. The gall.

Additionally, these ingenuous relatives overcompensated for inept children, believing their offspring brought more to the table than gross underachievement. That said, Shakes spent as much time as possible doing his own thing, out and about in the city and far afield from destructive family ties.

Even as a youngster Shakes paid close attention to actions much more than words, filing despotic observations away for future reflection. And at sixteen he figured a couple of things out:

1. My mother is being taken advantage of.

2. I'm all too glad to step away from family complexities not tied to basic compassion.

To sever the dysfunction he simply set out on his own, freeing himself from a retched whine concerning miniscule problems where solutions were rarely sought; where victimhood coupled with a false sense of self-importance and entitlement were the standard ethos. He walked away and didn't look back. Why look back at fools, those blind to other people outside their own pathetic existence; deaf to truths and facts, and immune to oft repeated verbal vomit while omitting past transgressions as if that tactic disguised abhorrent tendencies.

Shakes final thoughts regarding familial parasites: "Let the cunts be cunts to one another. I'll pass."

Craving independence, Shakes consistently worked some sort of job since the age of eleven: mowing lawns, delivering newspapers, learning to repair computers and write code, selling stolen skateboards, and selling a little weed here and there. With him, money and survival were not an issue, nor was couch surfing with friends and business associates and the occasional hookup.

Street-smart, intelligent and wary of most people, there were two key points imbedded in his mind; in a sense, lessons learned: depend on oneself in most situations and only turn to others for help when trust was not an issue. Everyone else could politely fuck off.

Regardless of Katie's situation, contacting Shakes was relatively easy if the proper order of ten numbers could be recalled. At times, however, for her, this proved difficult. So for simplicity sakes he purposely kept the same cell number—open to maternal contact whenever, wherever. He carried burner phones as well, disposables, depending on what line of business he was involved in at any given time.

Since early childhood he had inherently understood his mother's plight, feeling deeply the complicated hand Katie was dealt. Being judgmental and vile were traits he put on hold, allowing understanding and compassion to seep through when dealing with those less fortunate as others.

Education was something Shakes gravitated toward as well; more accurately, continuous education, whether it be classroom time (virtual or live), engaged person-to-person learning moments, online searches and videos, or reading a book, a manual, or an in-depth article. With a smartphone almost everything was at his fingertips, and, when not, it at least sought the path of warm direction. Moreover, he was no stranger to public libraries, comfortable in an atmosphere of whispers, ever enjoying the combined scent of mature paper and binding while surrounded by tall shelving and volumes of knowledge—tome cocoons.

Shakes found it amusing that a high percentage of those with proof of degree (a piece of thick-stock paper), considered themselves educationally worthy, educationally superior, even though they were usually in the education game for all the wrong reasons: ink printed on a framed document and an overpriced sweatshirt sporting school colors and fancy lettering. Ask the overwhelming majority of these walking collegiate billboards to elaborate off the top of their head on, say, pi squared, or a dangling participle, or the multiple languages spoken in Uzbekistan, and all you'd get in return would be a blank stare, the identical look directed at mommy when she raises her voice in a questioning tone regarding a suspicious liquor purchase on her credit card statement.

Nevertheless, Shakes respected true intellectuals, educated experts and truth seekers dedicating their lives to research, critical thinking, hard work and proof of knowledge; relying on facts while pushing aside unexamined opinions and fleeting fallacies—all the while welcoming change of thought when new evidence surfaced disproving old beliefs.

What most intrigued Johnny Blue while Shakes spoke was that the young man did not communicate like a typical eighteen-year-old. Far from it. His language was uncomplicated—pleasantly lacking a forced hipness—yet logically arranged and well relayed. Shakes was comfortable in a verbal fluidity canted toward a mature, polished realm.

He also refrained from rambling on, making intelligent, rational points without overselling what had just been said. He was efficient yet smooth with his articulation, giving actual thought to saying what he was about to say before saying it. This both impressed and embarrassed the career salesman; self-embarrassment.

The two had spent the better part of six hours in occupied conversation, with everything outside their blinders draped in mute darkness. They openly shared—verbally, nonverbally—being as honest as possible and discussing what needed to be discussed. A free flow of information.

They both now knew where the other stood and what they stood for. Beliefs. Thought processes. It was as if they'd experienced a thorough bureaucratic interview minus functionaries and a dreaded outcome.

The beginning of a team had formed, a duo, a connection, the way faithful friendships seem to happen. And they were off and running, a journey begun while engaged in an exciting venture with zero direction or boxed in thinking.

Nothing like catching a massive wave of excitement and adventure while lacking destination. A dangerous joyride. Figure it out by doing. Johnny Blue and Shakes Montoya were comfortable with the uncomfortability of change. Major change.

They set a date for a future rendezvous a month out. Prior to that, as in the following day, Blue would be jetting off to the Pacific Northwest for a brief stay before catching a second flight back to the Midwest. Once home, he'd rid himself of most personal possessions—unwanted clothes, condo, car, furniture, other useless stuff—while getting down to the bare essentials.

Eleven

Johnny Blue landed in Portland and headed straight for the rental car pavilion. Once in a vehicle he steered off airport property and drove north, destination known a two-hour drive away. Within minutes he was motoring across a concrete bridge, the Columbia river ebbing beneath, and soon crossed over into Clark County—the southernmost county in Washington State. He settled in at a cruise control speed of five miles an hour above the posted limit, slowly decompressing as passing populations decreased and anxieties subsided, thankful he was no longer trapped in a flying tube surrounded by pretzel-eating strangers.

The pleasant drive there seemed like a blink of an eye as Johnny exited the freeway and entered small-town Washington. The next twenty minutes had him navigating wet pavement with a recurring theme of dark patchwork. Occasionally eyeing the passing landscape, he witnessed signs of a decaying forest industry: a solitary barge moving raw lumber along the sound, floating logs corralled in a shallow cove.

At the last second—showing impeccable timing and skill— Johnny hung a hard left onto a steep gravel driveway engulfed in lush trees and greenery. Tapping down on the accelerator, he gassed the four-cylinder car to the top of a hill before leveling out into a broad clearing with a stunning view of the southwest portion of Puget Sound.

To his right, a house in decline sat perched atop a rise overgrown in thick foliage—a lone pickup abandoned amid fallen trees. Trash was strewn about; here and there, heaps, random untidiness. Johnny's first thought while observing the dilapidated dwelling and wrecked yard: meth house. His second and third thoughts: nature's volume, not soundless but agreeable.

As he stepped away from the car, nobody came from the house in greeting. This lack of welcoming did not surprise him in the least. He sensed occupancy, though, and swallowed hard as he approached a slightly open front door, fighting back a strong urge to vomit as foul odors pervaded roused senses.

He pinched his nose completely shut with his right thumb and index finger, then kneed the door wide open and gingerly straddled the threshold. He took in the entire front room—left, right, up, down. A king-size bed encircled by mounds of aging rubbish was the only piece of furniture in sight; an island surrounded by layered filth, with head of bed undistinguishable from foot of bed. And at one end of the bed, underneath a stained, frayed comforter, lay a motionless mass.

Not one to waste time, Johnny Blue dropped his right hand to his side, inhaled deeply through his mouth, braced himself in the doorway and let fly a series of high-pitched screams: HOOT, HOOT, HOOOOOOT! Several seconds later the dead lump came to life, slow motion like, while serving up a croaky grumble in retort, "You motherfucker." Then, a bit more movement—a jerky, stop-then-go totter—as the hidden figure began to claw at the comforter, searching for daylight and uncovered stale air.

Soon thereafter a foul smelling bear-like man appeared; hair and beard a jumbled mess. Struggling to sit up, a blurry eyed Rob Zamora looked over at Johnny Blue standing in the doorway, and said, "What the fuck are you doing here?"

Johnny: Wanted to make sure you weren't dead. And, if not, then I figured we could talk.

Rob: About what?

Johnny: Go clean yourself up, you smelly fuck. Then meet me outside. By the way, this place smells like ass, and you should answer your phone every once in a while, especially when it's fuck'n ringing.

Rob: How would you know what my ass smells like?

Johnny: Try actually listening, cheese-dick. I said ass, not your ass. But I'm guessing it is your dirty ass that's responsible for this mess. I'll give you an hour to clean up. That means take a shower and brush your teeth and put on the cleanest clothes you own, if that's even possible at this point.

Rob: It seems to me that your tone is not coming from a place of love, my friend.

Johnny: I wouldn't be here if I didn't love you, Rob. Now get up, you fat fuck. Is that enough love for you?

Rob: Oh, now I feel it. That is your love, especially the "fat fuck" part. I'll be out in an hour, fuck-stick. And don't let the door hit you on the ass.

After shutting the door, Johnny turned toward fresh air and headed for the car. He was smiling the biggest of smiles, a shit-eating grin, as he thought about exchanged insults between comrades. He was ecstatic that his ornery friend was still alive and kicking, and then he got in the rental car and headed into town.

Rob walked out of the house fifty-five minutes later, ahead of schedule and happy about it. Johnny was sitting on the rental car's hood alongside two cups of minimart coffee, the front bumper serving as a footrest. Rob eagerly eyed the rising steam coming from the Styrofoam cups.

He hadn't shaved because that would have been asking a lot. His clothes were ragged and dirty, even soiled, yet he felt alive again after showering for the first time since who knows when; reenergized due to soap, warm water, and a good old-fashioned scrubbing.

Rob was sporting all-black attire: baggy shorts, an oversized sweatshirt, and flip-flops with barely a sole—worn paper-thin. And as he made his way to the car in his all-black ensemble, Johnny Blue, oddly enough, couldn't help but be reminded of Johnny Cash.

He handed his old friend a large cup of coffee. Rob mumbled something unintelligible, removed the lid from the cup, and gently took a sip of hot black mud. A little while later, aided by a sip or three of strong java, he said, "Nothing like a cup of cheap burnt coffee to make you feel good again. Thanks, Johnny Blue."

Uttering his friend's name out loud for the first time in what seemed like too long ago (seeming like that because it was like that) sparked something deep within a mental reservoir. Suddenly Rob was overcome with emotion. It had been quite some time since he'd experienced human contact. The simple act of someone caring for him—speaking with him, buying him a cup a coffee, being barebones decent to him—had him on the verge of breaking down.

He fought back tears. And then he fought back a guttural groan that both surprised and frightened him. He was a bit confused, unable to comprehend what was going on internally.

Unsteady, he turned his back to Johnny Blue and inhaled deeply at an attempt to regain composure; hoping, praying, that he could pull it off. He did. Barely. For the time being, anyway, but only if he didn't have to look at Johnny Blue. Something about making eye contact with his longtime friend had him skirting a scary, psychological edge.

Johnny somehow understood the body language exhibited by Zamora; a complete comprehension within a fraction of the moment. Cued, he began to speak. He spoke for over two hours. And while he spoke, Rob did not turn around to face him. Not once.

Johnny Blue put it out there, his grand plan—the how's, the why's, the in-betweens. He unleashed what amounted to a business model of sorts to his one-man audience, having complete trust in the man standing across from him. Who has that? Johnny did.

From an admitted position of not knowing, he also spoke to his friend's pain, lost love, and the unsparing curveballs descending from the ether without reason. Rob, still facing away from his friend, nodded his head when prompted—for the most part up and down. But when Johnny served up strategic uncertainty, Rob remained still, waiting for precise strokes of clarity to eliminate ambiguities. In the end, they had an agreement. Whatever it takes, I'll be there for you in the form of action. I need something to live for.

Done proselytizing, Johnny stepped down from his rented soapbox—pushing off the car's hood and walking up behind his best friend. He put one arm around a broad shoulder and another around a muscled neck, clenching, squeezing, positioning his mouth at his friends left ear. "I love you, man. I really do. And I'm glad you're alive and that the band is back together again." Johnny released his hold after Rob let out a faint snicker, an instant before the first tremble.

Johnny walked back to the rental car, got inside, fired up the engine and headed north for Seattle. He had another plane to catch.

As he looked in the rearview mirror, he watched as his friend dropped to his knees while burying his face in his hands. Rob began shaking uncontrollably and crying like he'd cried at only one other time in his life—a lengthy, soul-searching cry.

Funny the emotional pain that roars to life from an unforeseen nudge.

Twelve

Rob Zamora spent a brief period mourning; and then, without delay, leapt headfirst into a monthlong frenzy tied to cleaning, painting, demolition, basic repairs, and landscaping. On top of that, he was hellbent on getting rid of shit that didn't matter while mowing shit down that was in the way. And by the time he'd wrapped things up; well, what once appeared to be a condemned house no longer existed due to extensive revamping and tons of debris removal.

He'd also cleaned up his food intake while committing to sufficient water consumption. With added exercise and a tweaked diet—sixteen-hour work days seven days a week—he dropped thirty-five pounds. Cranking it up a notch, he shaved, got a haircut, and bought new clothes: more black shorts, more black T-shirts, a black windbreaker, a black sweatshirt, a pair of black jeans, two pairs of black flip-flops and a pair of black sneakers with three pairs of black socks—each item fitted neatly inside a faded green duffel bag with room to spare.

Overdo for an internal tune-up, he went to the doctor and got a complete physical. After being poked and prodded and compared to a healthy ox, he met with a dentist to correct pesky oral hygiene issues. And with bodywork complete…

Voila! The new Rob Zamora looked nothing like his driver's license picture depicting a less than enthusiastic retired Marine—bloated, fat, depressed. With pronounced physical changes taking place, an unattached observer may have concluded that Zamora was preparing to reengage with members of the opposite sex. And they would have been dead wrong, because Rob was simply preparing to go back to work. Set to do what he did best.

Next up on Rob's list was to sell the house and sell the truck. They were no longer needed. In their place: a sixteen-foot Airstream travel trailer and an all-wheel drive sedan. He considered them necessities and arranged their purchase through a trusted confidant who was paid up front in cash as well as two thousand dollars over asking price for each item.

His friend was an oyster farmer who lived several miles down the road. And the old-time farmer, Oyster Joe, was the outright legal owner of Rob's new trailer and car. He then let Rob park both at the farthest edge of his property—in a distant corner with a private driveway. The two men had struck a deal, a deal sealed with a handshake. And the best part of their mutual pact: no questions asked, no answers needed.

Rob also purchased a used shipping container, a twenty-footer. He and Oyster Joe, with the assistance of a boom crane, set the container in place at an elevation higher and a yard or two in front of the Airstream trailer. So when viewed straight on from level ground, all you'd see in return was a red shipping container resting idle in a field not far from a dense grove. Also out of view was a covered car parked at the beginning of a gravel road that led into the woods.

Within the container—behind heavy-duty lock and key—Rob stored his remaining valuables: important documents, jewelry, mementos, artwork, and a small but efficient arsenal (four handguns, two rifles, a healthy supply of ammunition, a razor-sharp hunting knife). Rob's private stash didn't take up but a quarter of the container, with the remaining square footage used as a workshop.

Lastly, Rob closed out all personal accounts: bank, credit card, utility, and anything else remotely connecting him to an accurate residence. He performed a change of address as well, with his new forwarding address located in a small town in northeast Idaho close to the Montana border—a postal box belonging to a friend of a friend of a longtime acquaintance who'd gladly shred Rob's incoming junk mail for a onetime service fee of ten crisp one hundred-dollar bills.

Rob then placed close to three hundred thousand dollars in stacks of twenty-dollar denominations in Oyster Joe's floor safe, a safe sunk into thick reinforced concrete that rested beneath an expensive Persian rug in a secure, spotless, modern barn. And much more secure than your average bank vault, because Oyster Joe believed in high-tech security, two well-trained Belgian Malinois, and the right to bear arms—a shit-ton of arms.

Thirteen

The gravedigger works into the wee hours. Alone. The act of digging a grave is not exactly quiet, nor that loud, either.

A sub-compact tractor is involved, powered by a low-humming diesel engine. Its backhoe is the most valuable piece of equipment for the job. A sturdy shovel propped against a tree is at the ready, used to finetune the dig, to get to where the tractor's clawed bucket can't delicately get to. The goal at hand: a well dug grave.

The night animals certainly hear, feel, the goings on, but distance keeps humanity from absorbing even the loudest of sounds. Not that anyone would care that a grave was being dug—as long as it wasn't meant for them, of course.

You'd think that lowering one's body into a grave in the middle of the night with no one around would be a tad bit harrowing. Not for the gravedigger, feeling comfortable in tight quarters surrounded by dark earthy walls, with top of head—at its peak—inches below ground level. This is not an experienced gravedigger, but a first time gravedigger. Still, worry free, like a beach bum in Australia.

Once done, the gravedigger sits at grave's edge, at the end where head of body will eventually rest. Booted feet dangle inside the grave. An inspection is taking place, with a beam of light slowly combing squared, soil-packed walls—up then down, left then right. Looks good.

Now it's time to cover the grave with a rusted hunk of metal, bigger than the grave's opening and once part of a buoy tender's hull. Sturdy chains along with the tractor assist in dragging the dense slab of steel into place. Then, an effort to camouflage by scattering about surrounding groundcover. But not too much effort. Finally, an inconspicuous marker is hung high in a nearby tree.

The grave will be easily found by those who need to find it.

Fourteen

Shakes was standing outside a bus station in Grants Pass, Oregon, gulping down a bottle of overpriced water and staring at a logo of a really fast dog. At Johnny Blue's request, he agreed to travel to the Pacific Northwest to spend two weeks with Rob Zamora getting indoctrinated in a world foreign to him.

Shakes had openly admitted that he'd never traveled beyond California's borders, had only been outside San Francisco's city limits when absolutely necessary, as in you could count those rare occasions on a thumbless hand. Shakes remembered Johnny's words while inspecting freshly printed bus tickets just prior to departure: "You are about to expand your horizons, my friend." And then he laughed. Not Shakes, but Johnny.

After tossing the empty bottle in a nearby trash can, he walked around to the back of the bus, stopped, and took a healthy hit off a vape pen; not for a splash of nicotine but for a liberal dose of THC. Once back on the bus, he unzipped his backpack and removed a used copy of *Coming Through Slaughter*. Having read this book countless times, he now had a cannabis assist to induce a comfortable focus; downshifting to a lower gear, opening up to the poetic cadence of Ondaatje's writing.

Shakes read. Shakes slept. Shakes observed Oregon's geography, somewhat enamored by the overabundance of greenery. However, once the bus entered the state of Washington he became antsy, feeling out of his element as certain realizations began to sink in, like the one where he was about to spend two weeks with a friend of a friend—a perfect stranger, really.

He was nowhere near a comfort zone; far, far from familiarity. No worries, though, as he settled down in a neighborhood of new. This newness elevated excitement levels. It also heightened healthy fear levels, and Shakes chose to place his focus there while letting negativity wane. Above all, he was willing to learn new shit. He was willing to expand his skill set.

Late that night they pulled into a small bus station—more of a bus stop than an actual station. The driver steered the forty-five-footer between two white lines, parking in a bus-sized stall. Shakes had arrived. Time to get off.

He stood outside shooting the breeze with a group of fellow passengers. They were waiting for the retrieval of luggage stored in the bus's underbelly—underneath floorboards where thousands of soles had tapped about. Inside his roller bag: clothes, shoes, skateboard, helmet, toiletries. Shakes had stored valuable electronic equipment in his backpack: phone, pad, videocam, cords, chargers.

He looked around but didn't see anybody who he thought might be Zamora. Finally, from his left, at borderline periphery, he heard, "Yo, Shakes, let me get one of those bags."

Shakes turned and looked as the former military man approached. He wasn't tall. He wasn't short. He didn't appear old or young. He wasn't overly muscular—not the leaned-out version of Zamora—and not the type of dude that stood out in a crowd. But what he was, was athletic.

Shakes had spent countless hours around skateboarders, street break-dancers, grapplers. He knew athletic when he saw athletic. He knew wiry strong when he saw that too. And he especially knew fluid movement when it strode his way.

Shakes' thoughts were validated once Zamora leaned in to shake his hand. He wasn't the corporate dickhead type who tries to crush your hand in an attempt to prove a worthless point. It was a different experience altogether. Rob knew exactly how much pressure to apply while offering up just a taste of his overall strength, maybe thirty percent at the most. On top of that, Zamora had large, large hands, hands that belonged at the end of an NBA forward's long sinewy forearms.

Shakes felt at ease with Rob from initial contact. Zamora was a laid-back dude. Shakes was a laid-back dude. They didn't force anything: conversation, communication, not one thing. They both let the world come to them, as if there was any other way.

Ten minutes into the ride home, Rob caught Shakes' attention as he greatly reduced vehicle speed and turned toward forest. Within seconds they were motoring down a veiled road surrounded by heavy thicket—tires crunching tiny rocks while headlights illuminated greenish-brown limbs that lightly fingered the vehicle's exterior. They eventually stopped at the end of a gravel road, not far from a travel trailer, not far from a shipping container. It was late and semi-dark, a bright half-moon perched high in the sky.

Zamora let Shakes have the trailer as his personal suite. He believed in being a proper host and had no problem sleeping in the shipping container; on a cot, doors propped wide open, with his temporary bed draped in mosquito netting. He'd slept in worse. Much worse.

Wide awake they were before six in the morning, watching as the morning light spread, as the day brightened. No rush in getting up, yet no point in staying in bed. Rob started the coffee process, pouring water into a gooseneck kettle, placing it over a flame, and prepping the coffee and filter for eventual pour over.

The next two weeks unfolded like Shakes thought they would, and, opposite initial expectations, also unfolded completely different in an altogether unanticipated direction. They worked long hours, long days. No surprise there. Shakes was educated on new disciplines, new concepts, but, believe it or not, also played the role of educator. And this he had not foreseen.

Zamora was as interested in Shakes and what he brought to the table, so to speak, as he was introducing tried, effective training methods to the younger man. An additional surprise Shakes encountered was that Zamora focused on teaching but a very limited subject matter. Rob was more interested in getting things right— redundant with instructional content and redundant in practical application—as in let's do it over and over and over again. Now let's apply what we've learned by training it in the dark on a feel only basis. Educate self by doing yet keeping it simple.

The two-week stay seemed to fly by in an instant, with Shakes enjoying every minute spent in the Northwest. They both learned a great deal during their educational retreat. In truth, they gained more than expected. They gained friendship. And as Shakes extended a hand to Zamora at the very same bus station where they'd met fourteen days prior, he was completely surprised when Rob ignored his gesture and stepped in for a bro hug.

As Rob squeezed a bit too hard, Shakes did his best to reciprocate—feeling for the first time the brute strength that the older man possessed. After breaking their embrace, after they both stepped back in slight embarrassment, Shakes sincerely thanked Rob for his time and hospitality. Rob, at a loss for words, offered up an understanding nod just prior to Shakes boarding the bus.

And as the bus drove away, Zamora felt the piercing pangs of loneliness.

Fifteen

Johnny Blue was driving in comfort and feeling like a retiree, as in he looked the part of an old codger from the Midwest. A visual he detested.

After selling almost everything, he had cash to burn. So he purchased an Airstream Atlas Touring Coach, dropping $225K on the bad dog of all bad dogs in the motorhome universe. Why? Because it was now his new home, his new form of transportation, and his new office/recording studio—an all-inclusive unit with quite an assortment of bells and whistles.

Johnny banked half of his remaining cash in an easy access account, with the other half stashed in a secure compartment concealed inside the motorhome. He wasn't interested in interest. He was interested in access.

After driving from Nebraska to California, he arrived back in San Francisco one foggy Friday morning to meet up with an accomplished civil rights attorney from a near forgotten era, a gentleman whose client list also included an array of characters from the organized crime world, the anarchist/eco-terrorist world, and the free speech movement world—if there's still such a thing (there is). This lawyerly fellow, Lawyer Bill, had done a solid job at keeping a high percentage of clients from spending long stretches of time behind bars when the government and its many tentacles advocated lengthy prison sentences and quiet control of these so-called enemies of the state.

Johnny's newfound legal representation wasn't cheap, but effective, as in it was swathed in experience and a proven track record. Lawyer Bill was without a doubt a high-end insurance policy that gave Johnny Blue peace of mind—just in case and you never know. His new attorney was also convincing from a dominant presence point of view: big in stature, verbose, well dressed, and as smart as a whip with a streetfighter's moxie.

Age wise, Lawyer Bill was somewhere in his seventies and would probably refute reasonable odds and live another twenty years or so while still plowing through eighty-hour workweeks and attacking life like a rock star. Johnny joked that the old-time litigator would officially exit this world on the cusp of a century lived while juggling a top-tier blowjob, a glass of strong Kentucky bourbon, and the pungent smoke of a handcrafted Corona Gorda cigar. Johnny Blue was infatuated with Lawyer Bill's zest for life, craft, booze, tobacco, and erotic adventure. A long-lost breed indeed.

After leaving the downtown area, Johnny drove to the outskirts of the city for his second meeting of the day. He found parking close to the ocean, not an easy find in a motorhome—not an easy find, period. Ten minutes later there was a knock, knock, knock on the side door. It was Shakes, with skateboard and backpack in tow.

"Come in," shouted Blue.

Shakes did as told, opening the door, peeking inside, and saying, "Very nice, I think I'll get one," as he laughed and stepped up into the impeccably engineered house on wheels.

Blue and Shakes jumped into a lengthy conversation concerning two separate subject matters:

1. Speaking tour scheduling.

2. The video and audio innerworkings related to live events and podcasts.

They were about to venture into virgin territory by producing their own content in two different formats and putting it out there for the world to absorb. Johnny would be relying heavily on Shakes for technical savvy and internet upload, both mainstream and the dark web. Johnny's responsibilities lie with research, content and presentation. He would be out in front of the camera while Shakes peered through its lens, playing an integral role behind the scenes.

As they steered toward conclusion—after working through production details and estimating future costs—Johnny switched topics and asked Shakes a question about men's clothing. Shakes, caught off guard, looked directly at Blue to make sure he wasn't about to have his weenie yanked on with 60-grit sandpaper. Once convinced the question was of a serious nature, he directed Johnny toward a website that specialized in skate/punk/surf wear, with an emphasis on dark colors.

Johnny bit. A modern, comfortable wardrobe was on the horizon. All he needed now was access to an Amazon locker in the city linked to not so difficult parking, a must for home delivery when your home is mobile. He would find what he was looking for at a grocery store in the Marina.

When Shakes stepped from the motorhome and began skating away, he had a quicker spin to his roll. He felt alive. He felt motivated. He felt like life really mattered. For the first time in a long time—maybe the first time ever—he felt as if immersed in purpose.

Johnny Blue was also submerged in cause, now spending countless hours studying and rehearsing. He routinely practiced his verbal timing—over and over—sometimes out loud standing in front of a mirror, sometimes in a whisper while lying in bed. He prepared and prepared and prepared some more, endlessly.

He hustled—on foot, door to door—finally landing a speaking gig at a small church in the city. He would speak to a live audience the day after he and Shakes recorded their first podcast, and probably to a small group of parishioners uninterested in what he had to say. It didn't matter. The time to preach was now.

No more than thirty minutes speaking was his goal—quality minutes not quantity minutes. Johnny Blue understood audience attention spans, often reciting old advice freely handed down early on in his sales career: "A lot of public speakers miss the mark when it comes to audience awareness. They get trapped by their own ego. They get caught up in hearing their own voice, as if a barrage of words assists with comprehension. Sales people, if worth their weight in precious metal, understand the art of getting to the point in a reasonable amount of time and doing so with conviction."

And upon that day's arrival, that special day, Johnny Blue was more than ready and more than willing to share his message with the masses. The day prior, a podcast had been recorded and uploaded to the universe. He and Shakes had successfully pulled off their first show without a hitch.

It was time to do what he'd been preparing for. He parked a good mile away, choosing to walk and think before speaking. Shakes would not be attending, which meant the event would not be recorded. For Johnny, his one and only dress rehearsal.

He was decked out in the new look—all black. And as he arrived at the church carrying a stack of pink bakery boxes with five dozen malasadas neatly arranged inside, he felt that familiar twinge in his lower gut. He was ready to give the performance of a lifetime.

With sugary, doughy treats and hot cups of coffee occupying aged hands, the congregants—roughly fifty older black men and women, mostly women—eyed the unknown white boy making his way toward the podium at the front of the church. Johnny would not be using the podium, instead leaving it as a backdrop. He wanted zero barriers between speaker and audience. He coveted vulnerability with nowhere to hide, forcing an inherent honesty.

Go.

He began by speaking to the ineptitude of the two major political parties—the Democrats, the Republicans—and their inability to work in harmony while doing their best to discredit the other.

"The two biggest political parties in this country are nothing more than marketing slogans, slogans that accomplish very little and rarely benefit the masses, with their suited representatives droning on and on about the same old rehearsed talking points. They are no different than their predecessor's irritating hum from generations past."

He also spoke to shared alliances between the two parties, citing times throughout history where they appeared to work as one— but only for political favor—as they rationalized wars, racism, gender inequality, the stymieing of progress on certain basic human rights and, of course, a capitalistic economy based on gross overconsumption.

"Their disingenuous spin is tied to horrific deeds disguised as acts of patriotism. And if against them, a single word uttered in defiance, then you, my friend, are the antithesis of patriotism and will be quickly labeled as the bad word of the day: unpatriotic, communist, radical, socialist, fascist, collaborator, terrorist, or whatever shameful word gains the most attention. '*Sticks and stones may break my bones, but nasty words spoken against me by people in power cause far, far worse repercussions.*'"

He then pointed out a falsehood shared by both parties, that one party is good and the other bad. "Regardless of mainstream political affiliation, the hierarchy of both major parties—if listened to and watched closely—can never be trusted because that trust was purchased long ago."

When speaking to capitalism and overconsumption and how this economic model is contrary to the good of the planet—to the good of the world's citizens—and that it is beyond inefficient, he gladly gave a clear-cut example of this inefficiency by pointing out that "there are six empty houses to every one homeless person in the United States alone."

And on the subject of planet survival, instead of just knocking the "Right" regarding their "ignorance and deceitful rhetoric surrounding this catastrophic matter," he also took a jab at the "Left" by pointing out their "false agreements with other countries tied to global warming, where proof of lackluster results meant nothing because no real penalties are dished out when agreed upon standards aren't met. Simply put, both parties pretend to fight for the commoners as they flout basic legal and ethical standards so as to benefit the powerful and the wealthy. One and the same, really."

Blue's solution based point, his magic elixir tying everything together in the name of change: "Radical action gets results. An unpredictable dose of radical action forces people in power to lessen their grip while placing a wet finger in the air to see which way the wind is blowing."

And he gave examples of change tied to slavery and race turmoil—the main morale and economic issues leading up to the Civil War; examples of labor unions being formed and eventually taking hold in the late nineteenth and early twentieth centuries due to worker abuse and repulsive working conditions; examples of radicals in the 1960s and 70s who were fed up with racism, war, and gender and economic inequality—people that truly forced change but were then eliminated, imprisoned, or forced to fade away to a forgotten corner for survival purposes.

He spoke to the avoidance of joining groups. Instead, stressing the smarter path of acting alone or in small, trusted circles. He used LOAF as an example from an ideological and self-preservation standpoint. LOAF was still up and running decades after forming, with no leaders and but a few basic rules where individuals were forced to own up to their actions because they were self-led. Imagine that, self-leadership.

"The problem with groups, organizations and clubs is that they can be compromised, easily infiltrated. Ask historians in the know why most radical groups that existed during desperate times of change have all but vanished. Where did they go? The sad answer to that question revolves around their 'elimination,' where they were internally or externally wiped out; mismanaged, imploded, or destroyed from the outside by any means necessary. Eaten alive by power and wealth. Again, one and the same."

Johnny then stressed that life has very few organic rules. "An overabundance of unnatural rules—manmade laws, manmade doctrine—were invented by control mongers so as to maneuver advantages their way." This last statement causing the preacher in the far reaches of the room to raise a fatherly eyebrow.

Blue offered a factual point of view, with all statistical information used easily found on-line or, when requested, handed out in leaflet form at the end of a presentation—showing exactly where he sourced pertinent data. He pleaded to be challenged with facts and ideas, however farfetched.

And when legitimate opposing information came his way causing a change in thought or opinion, then he would do just that. He was not forced into any one ideology, nor did he believe that anyone else should be limited in scope. Johnny Blue's messaging was based on facts and critical thinking; thus, he was open to change, self-change.

Additionally, Blue let the congregation know that his presentation was not based on original thought. Instead, it was based on order of thought, as he stated, "I arranged a belief system around successful actions taken by brave souls during historical periods where actual change occurred for those but a microscopic dot in conventional power's rearview mirror. And, most important, where the right thing got done—something most world leaders rarely pull off."

In closing, he delivered an ardent argument against violence, against mayhem, in that it was not something he would personally engage in. But on the flipside of that slippery disc, he made the point that he wouldn't preach to anyone in terms of what they should or should not do in the fight for social change.

Johnny looked at himself as a messenger of change, leaving the method of change or the thing to be changed up to the change agents themselves; those willing to act on whatever change they deemed necessary. A free for all in thinking and action was what he proposed. Let change begin.

Johnny spoke ten minutes longer than planned and was already contemplating where to trim the wordy fat before his next speaking engagement four days hence. But exiting straightaway he did not. The congregation was an astute, experienced lot and not prone to ignore personal duty when advice and counterargument were ready to be dished out. Five modishly attired parishioners were standing in wait to meet with Johnny Blue. He would be there for an additional two hours.

Johnny was schooled, guided, loved, admonished. It's what he needed. It's what he wanted. Growth was his main goal. But he also craved a dose of validation, however small.

The first person to approach Johnny was an older gentleman wearing an impeccably tailored tan suit and holding a malasada in his left hand. While shaking Johnny's hand, he asked about the donut-like item in his other hand. Johnny Blue, caught off guard and misinterpreting the man's question, overcompensated and replied with far too much information regarding the Portuguese confection. The older gentleman, a study in profound patience and only wanting to know the whereabouts of the shop where the donuts were purchased, nodded as if in understanding, but really to extinguish further explanation because he'd heard enough. Then, he purposely made direct eye contact with Johnny Blue, taking on a serious, engaged look and immediately gaining the younger man's attention.

"Why did you decide to speak with us?" he asked, spreading his arms wide in reference to his fellow congregants.

Johnny replied in a respectful manner, saying that the good reverend of the church was the first person of many asked who allowed him time, place, and audience. Most others asked declined his request.

"Did you know that you would be speaking to an all-black audience?"

Johnny said that he assumed the audience members would be mostly black, but not one hundred percent black.

The gentleman smiled, adding, "Throughout our history— after being shipped over here against our collective will—we've experienced the harsh political realities you speak of far more than any other race except for indigenous people? You do know that, correct?"

Johnny said that he was well aware of that fact but couldn't truly relate to it since he was a white dude from the suburbs who grew up in relative comfort. Adding that his approach, his pitch, was from a position of class struggle regardless of race. Johnny went on to say that he wasn't wealthy by any means, but doing well when compared to most and currently unemployed and living off personal savings. He went on to say that his intentions were genuine, and, until recently— due to not caring rather than not knowing—he'd become much more aware of obvious economic discrepancies associated with capitalism that are just flat-out counterproductive in every which way imaginable. Ending with, "Does that make any sense?"

The older gentleman, still smiling, said, "Thank you for your candor. I wish you luck in your endeavors. But more than that, I hope that you're not just another conman—another white conman from a history of conmen—who's hellbent on making a ruckus and then parlaying that babel into money, accolades, and fifteen minutes of fame. Because if that is what you represent, then I pray for your failure. But if you stay true to your intentions, and I'm giving you the benefit of the doubt in that area, then I pray for your success. But just remember this, if you do reach this level of success I speak of, success that I can envision, then it might not work out so well for you personally. But at least your conscience will be clear.

"Oh, and a few final points: You speak well. You have a good rhythm about you. And, you're easily understood. My last point—and I never thought I'd say this—get out there and speak to a much wider audience sprinkled with many more shades of white. Godspeed, young man."

And with that he shook Johnny's hand and bid him goodbye.

Over the next ninety minutes, Johnny spoke with three other congregants, all women, before the fourth church member, also a lady, approached. As he looked her way, then directly at her, he could not determine age. She could have been fifty, but was probably much older than that, moving with a dancer's grace—light on her feet—with high cheekbones and the black skin of an angel: perfect, flawless, dark chocolate brown.

She asked Johnny to take a seat; they would sit side by side. Johnny waited until she sat first, and she acknowledged this polite gesture with a tilt of the head in his direction. Once both were seated, she began with a deliberate manner of speech directed toward getting to the point without unnecessary discourse. University educated throughout the 1960s, she possessed a decades-enriched, adept vocabulary that she would be dumbing down for Johnny's benefit.

"Interesting sermon. Let me ask you a few questions: Are you familiar with The Zeitgeist Movement? Peter Joseph? Or his book, *The New Human Rights Movement*? Does any of this ring a bell?"

Shaking his head left then right then left again, Johnny said, "No." Then asked, "And your name is?"

"Ruth," she replied, before moving on.

"Let me suggest that you purchase and read the book I just mentioned. You will benefit by its relatively current publication and the accurate statistical data associated with it, to include exactly when and where this data was obtained. Also, the author does a good job of explaining 'structural violence.' And I'm going to assume that you've never heard of this term. Is that assumption correct?"

"Yes, it is," replied Johnny Blue.

"Good. Start there. It's not complicated, and it will enlighten you on subject matters you probably already know about but where you're intellectually lacking with regard to how widespread and truly devastating they are. And when I say devastating, I'm talking about millions of people dying each year due to poverty, with their respective deaths easily avoided if powerful political and corporate leaders cared enough about preventing such deaths. Quick stat: The World Health Organization shows that the number three killer of our citizenry in low-income countries is diarrheal related disease. That's right, Mr. Blue, death by one's own watery excrement. I don't know about you, but unnecessary deaths associated with mothers and fathers and their babies tends to make me upset."

"I'll get the book and read it," said Johnny.

She continued, "There was a huge tsunami in Indonesia about fifteen years ago. Do you remember that event?"

"I do."

"Just under a quarter of a million people perished in something like fourteen different countries. My numbers aren't exact, but I know I'm in the general statistical vicinity. Let me ask you this: Did any of those deaths affect you?"

"No, not in the least," replied Johnny.

"Good, you're being honest with me. My point is this: Millions of people die each year in countries we refer to as 'Third World' or low-income countries. Countries that rich, powerful nations have exploited for centuries. And their deaths don't impact us in the least. Because just like those people in Indonesia, we don't directly witness these atrocities. We don't feel their deaths at all. We get wind of deathly occurrences—a mere blip on the radar, per se—but not near enough graphic imagery to cause action or outrage. We have become personally detached; completely detached in my opinion.

"Think of the most horrible person or persons or groups throughout history who have been responsible for known genocides where millions of lives were purposely wiped out—Genghis Kahn, Columbus, the Three Pashas, Hitler, Stalin, Pol Pot, to name a few. These known monsters don't statistically come close to the millions of lives lost every year by what amounts to citizenry murder tied to turning a blind eye on poverty, with its death tally increasing by the second.

"And here's what you'll hear from those who act the part of caring citizen, who act the part of liberal or religious do-gooder: 'I didn't know. And what could I have done anyway?' So, they do nothing. The overwhelming majority of citizenry does nothing. I mention this because you mentioned it with respect to political leaders. What I'm telling you is that capitalism has failed the masses in a far greater way than you speak of. You are not truthful or radical enough for me, Mr. Blue.

"The people who benefit from capitalism are the very same on the left, the right, the middle, who act as if they care with words and words alone. Oh sure, they puff out their chests and stand behind do-little charities while giving their peers and supporters the artificial means to say what great people they are. And when they're issued lifetime achievement awards to make it look like they've performed godly deeds, they act surprised, even acting as if they know what humble really looks like.

"But that miniscule fraction of good waved about is a front to disguise their inherent getting over on those with little to nothing and who are dying in their own feces. And the middleclass and the upper middleclass play their puppet-like roles, being pushed and pulled and prodded to repeat the core message of the day. They are all hired shills, whether they know it or not.

"If you're serious, Mr. Blue, about what I think you want to change, then do more reading, do more research—quickly—and turn into a much more radical individual than you are right now. Get dirty and dig down to the ugly root of the matter. And once you find it, speak the truth from a perspective drenched in facts. Because right now you're just a little radical, what I call vanilla radical. All you qualify for in my book is a millimeter to the left of mainstream everything, sounding like every other aspiring talking head, if you catch my drift.

"Also, follow contemporary topics of debate from both Noam Chomsky and Dr. Cornel West, paying close attention to what they are speaking to and writing about.

"Plus, there are two women I would like to turn you on to as well: Angela Davis and Abbey Martin. With Angela Davis, focus on the history of her educational journey, both here and abroad, and the philosophical tenet she leaned toward. And with Abbey Martin, watch her online news program, *The Empire Files*, especially when she covers topics originating elsewhere such as the current political unrest in Venezuela and who's truly responsible for that turmoil. Compare their messaging with the establishment media messaging, and then compare them all with the truth.

"And lastly, focus on Dr. King's central theme of economic inequality, especially what he spoke to in 1968 leading up to his trip to Memphis."

Johnny, scribbling notes on a borrowed piece of paper, said, "I've definitely heard of most of those people."

"Good," said Ruth. "Now get on with it, young man. Time's wasting."

As he walked back to the rolling house on wheels, his head was spinning, his heart was racing, his spirit was as high as an untethered kite. He was facing a boatload of research, a monumental task cramped into a tight window of time that had him feeling like he was under the influence of drugs.

Johnny Blue was riding an adrenaline rush, something he'd rarely felt without the assistance of powerful powder. However, this new, natural drug was far better than the old method of getting high, and he now possessed a full realization of what men and women of the cloth refer to as "a calling."

But Johnny's calling wasn't connected to the misrepresentation of fear based fiction while taking followers' money and benefiting taxwise due to nonprofit status. His calling was the real deal, and Johnny Blue was convinced of his righteous standing. He was on the right track. The only track to be on.

Sixteen

True colors can sometimes be distorted. It really depends on the lens they're observed through, with many a lens blurred by hazy film.

"We are all subject to manipulation, to include the smartest streetwise hustler there ever was," Zamora said to Shakes, as they skillfully climbed an eighty-foot tree. Shakes often wondered why Rob blurted out what he blurted out. And, more times than not, he was prone to do just that; verbal bursts of wisdom from distant leftfield. Seldom were they nonsensical; but rather, purposely delivered with desired effect—intended to stay put, to be remembered, to be stored in a mental toolbox for later use.

It surprised him that he continued to remember his time spent with Zamora, vividly. And when considering Rob's spoken words, Shakes' recall—more often than not—bordered on verbatim. Many months had passed, but he remembered more today than he seemed to have remembered from back then. It was like life was unfolding in prearranged scenarios validating Zamora's wisdom firsthand. And Rob would never take credit for that wisdom, wouldn't consider it in the least, saying that it reveals itself to those willing to listen, see, feel.

Shakes was standing on a corner in San Francisco waiting for Johnny Blue to drive by and pick him up. Their destination was at the end of a lengthy drive up into faraway Northern California, to an event off the beaten path in remote Shasta County. Johnny had been booked to speak at a punk/bluegrass festival, with Shakes recording a portion of the event.

If Johnny's speaking career—his popularity—was a snowball, it was now rolling down a steep grade from high elevation, gaining momentum and growing with each revolution. Why? Who knows why? Right place, right time? Maybe.

Why do some new fashion shifts—new ideologies, new technology tweaks, new art forms—take off and cascade worldwide versus dying a quick death like most forced trends, ideas, and supposed newfound breakthroughs? Nobody really knows the answer to that question until well after the fact. And that is why pop culture, or culture in general, is consistently formulaic across a wide variety of spectrums.

Formulaic is predictable. Unimpressive, but predictable. And much easier to profit from. There is little rhyme or reason as to why fresh, unpredictable trends leap onto the scene and take hold, thus the words "fresh & unpredictable." But if they survive for a significant amount of time, then they, too, become predictable.

Truth told, Johnny was gaining momentum in quite a few circles, to include a partial sniff from one or two mainstream media outlets. But Johnny Blue wasn't interested in becoming the establishment flavor of the month, not wanting to assist in legitimizing this lesser form of ad-driven, wannabe journalism before fading away as fast as he'd arrived. He was astutely aware that he controlled his own destiny. And he was going to continue to do just that along with select, trusted partnerships. With Johnny Blue it came down to effort, trust, discipline, and truth. As well as a grassroots, online and in-person presence.

Then, from out of the blue, he got what he wanted. Big-time change.

Without so much as a warning, Johnny Blue crossed a line—a line drawn in the sand yet hidden by shadows—a crossing over that thrust him into the spotlight. He had started a campaign to eliminate idiot boxes (as in televisions) from as many households as possible. He'd preached this minimalistic concept during many speeches and podcasts. And for some odd reason this nonnew idea took on a life of its own while generating a bit of a hoopla. Soon enough, a day was selected to celebrate the ridding of household TVs, a day in May, to include parting ways with related cable and satellite services.

What Johnny had not anticipated was the number of households that would jump on the TV bashing bandwagon. What at first appeared to be a petty ploy, rapidly grew into a beast with teeth.

The initial push was for a million people to take the idea seriously, with a hopeful goal landing somewhere in the vicinity of one-tenth that number.

But what actually happened, what nobody saw coming, was that a little over three and a half times the original figure—with most of that taking place in the United States—joined in. Simply put, three-point-five-million-plus people (and counting) accepted the challenge. And this unforetold outcome put Johnny within earshot of the echoing establishment media mewl, which was both a good and not so good position to be in depending on one's perspective.

A large number of people began taking notice, to include the U.S. government, the conventional media, and corporate America. The bottom line: Some dude living in a van, traveling throughout America, reaching large audiences—both online and in living color—had just directly affected the country's economy, however slight, to include influencing a good chunk of people scattered across five separate continents. To quote one high ranking government official while speaking with the CEO of a major Cable TV conglomerate, "Who the fuck is Johnny Blue?"

Johnny now had a bright, freshly drawn target on his back, and he needed to come to grips with that fact because this thing he was doing, whatever it was, had become much bigger than him. And there were gaggles of self-important types who did not like the look, vibe, or swagger of one Johnny Blue.

Wise enough to know that celebrity is fleeting, Mr. Blue doubled down by increasing his workload and pushing for an even larger audience. His drive was that of quality, result-driven busy. And he was duly rewarded because of his efforts.

Time to be bold. Time to push on. Time to ignore the envious, the judgmental.

Not giving in to traditional media requests made Johnny Blue a hot commodity in opposing circles: mainstream versus alternative. Ignoring the norm pissed off those siding with the conventional lot, but, on the other hand, it was paying large dividends in growing his message globally with unconventional stalwarts. His self-confidence beamed right track, yet he was wisely cautious of fame.

And as he straddled the two-headed notoriety monster, he focused on keeping his ego in check—not wanting to get caught up in the myriad of compliments raining down from supporters, nor snagged by the viscous venom disgorged by detractors. He would ride the surf mid-wave, hopefully keeping the charging sharks and the mighty reef below at bay.

In full protection mode of Johnny Blue, Lawyer Bill enjoyed telling presumptuous news executives, "No." It also made his day when he didn't let pressing parties off easy with one word replies: No way, Jose. They got the full, verbal brunt of what they deserved whether they wanted to hear it or not.

Bill liked to inform the pompous media brass attempting to court his client that they weren't big enough at this point in the count-your-followers social media game. They'd arrived much too late to the party. Facts were, Johnny Blue had built a larger global audience than all the major news networks combined. Technology had passed them by with most people under the age of sixty. In the new technological world, nobody needed them anymore. Nobody.

When standing tall at the pulpit on live TV, Bill would not let up. "To say that the major TV networks produce fake news is not fair to them or to the satire enriched world that toys about with contrived news. What they really produce is partial, cherrypicked news. Not so much fake, but much worse—as in lacking. That's right, lacking news. Lacking in substance, research, critical thinking, complete truths and, above all, the heart of old-school journalism.

"Where have all the old-timey journalists gone? Journalists from another era like, say, a Hersh, a Safer, a Mohr. Those journalists from yesteryear who possessed souls, who wouldn't dare appear on late night TV talk shows to engage in predetermined back scratching with the invariably joking, affable host sitting elevated behind a desk.

"Current, up to speed, newfangled talking heads are spoiled children, with their fragile egos needing constant stroking. They win awards for reading basic English off a teleprompter, and for repeating the words 'Breaking News' after those exact words are barked into their earpiece by a voice sitting in a distant control room. Real journalists don't have time for that nonsense because they're working long meaningful days, long consequential weeks, long productive months, and long relevant careers.

"The major news networks put forth human robots sporting caked on makeup and tight designer clothing, where they bat around opinion after worn-out opinion with a repeated lineup of supposed expert panelists—all hoping that their meaningless opined shit (thank God for seven-second live TV delays) somehow sticks to a false wall. The only difference between the major news networks is content slant; and all at the direction of ownership and paid advertisers."

With the help of Lawyer Bill, Johnny Blue was gaining followers and enemies—enemies with money and power.

PART II

It was the comedian George Carlin who said, "Power does what power wants."
Spoken words that could not ring truer; and, without a punchline.

Seventeen

Power set in motion the beginning of the end to an unnerving possibility. It started as an investigation; an investigation stirred from the bowels of a dungeon of lies. Take your time, perform due diligence, be thorough, fair, transparent—the buzz words of the day that didn't mean diddly-squat. It's important for those in positions of power to tee it up properly before commencing the fucking over of whomever. It has to sound right—seem correct, of course it's true—when coming from a position of righteous damnation. No different than a gutless autocrat, the lies have to be believable among the unseeing, fearful followers.

The initial contact did not surprise him in the least. It was part of the job and something he'd been expecting because the gap between assignments had been longer than usual. So when the package appeared at the drop-off point, he felt an internal jump-start of sorts. And after reviewing the file on who they wanted him to take a serious look at, well—a sideways tilt of the head—that did catch him slightly off balance because he had actually heard of the guy.

It wasn't that he didn't have knowledge of those they directed him toward. He knew more than not. What seemed odd to him was that this man was currently in the public eye; very much so, and a lightweight when compared to the usual cadre of characters he routinely dealt with. In his world normal was a terrorist—a mobster, a spy, a sworn enemy—your basic garden-variety underworld types that nobody really cares about or remembers once gone.

And to make a point, Nolan would sometimes ask wisenheimers thought to be well-versed in worldly matters this simple question: Off the top of your head, name one of the six convicted terrorists behind the bombing of the World Trade Center North Tower in 1993?

Crickets.

Crickets.

Crickets.

James Nolan sat patiently over a sugary cup of coffee and the scattered contents from a linen envelope. After finishing his second cup of coffee, he concluded that his contemplative efforts were complete. Bottom line, he was done analyzing and ready to go to work. The former Marine sniper—currently working for an obscure agency within the federal government whose compacted title was yet another tired acronym—was about to head out on a work-related trip bound for the West Coast. His only hesitation: the easy feel of the job, with zero complications jutting out on the horizon. It was a basic op, and James Nolan despised basic anything. In spite of lackluster feelings, he would soldier on.

Arriving in San Francisco under one of many aliases, Nolan rented a car and drove toward a townhall meeting located twenty-five miles southeast of the airport. After crossing the San Mateo bridge he entered the city of Hayward—a bedroom community with a blue-collar vibe. And after two right turns and a few miles of road in between, he found the meeting site across the street from a liquor store on Mission Boulevard, a church property situated amid an unexceptional neighborhood.

After entering the lot, he parked as far from the church as possible; simple reasoning, limited options and a quick exit, settling for a spot between a net-less hoop and a set of concrete steps leading up to an unkept baseball diamond. The parking lot was filled with an assortment of vehicles, to include a pair of washed-out yellow school buses. A few stragglers were walking toward the church hall, which also doubled as a gymnasium.

Reminiscent of the 1960s, there sat an aging Catholic church and grade school; Saint something or other. A scattering of unattached, ill-assorted buildings stood at random locations: two classroom wings over here, the gymnasium over there, the church with attached rectory constructed by a side street, and what appeared to be a convent arbitrarily stuffed just outside the sandlot's leftfield fence. All built on a large plot of land back when plenty of land could be had.

Not an ounce of architectural thought or logic had been taken into account after the church and rectory were erected. And as he got out of the rental car—wearing unfashionable glasses, a bland baseball cap, and a relatively new but inexpensive coat—James thought, 'You could build an entire fucking neighborhood on this slab of asphalt. What a waste.'

Nobody noticed Nolan when he entered the hall and walked over to the coffee urn. Nobody paid attention as he grabbed a seat in the middle of the chattering throng and sipped from a cup of nasty coffee while nibbling on an even nastier stale donut. And nobody took note of his exit when he sauntered out of the hall at the conclusion of Johnny Blue's discourse, an empty Styrofoam cup and a single napkin occupying his left hand. Rarely did anybody take interest in James Nolan, and he relished in that fact.

He finally saw and heard what he came to see and hear, up close, within forty feet. He was not impressed, nor could he grasp the phenomenon of one Johnny Blue. Sure, the guy could speak. And sure, he handled himself better than most, especially when compared to the talking heads and politicians and corporate types that appear often enough on TV. But that wasn't saying much, now was it?

'Speaking of TVs,' Nolan thought, 'maybe that's the reason why everybody's in such an uproar. Or is it because this Johnny Blue character has the ability to attract people to his cause. Who knows?' Then he thought, 'At least wait the guy out and see if he can get another three million converts to drink the purple Kool-Aid. Please do that before wasting any more of my time by flying me around the country and forcing me to attend townhall meetings where the coffee tastes like goat piss.'

As he drove away, he was internally thanking himself for not squandering away additional time, probably an entire day, by committing to countersurveillance measures at the onset of the job. He had certainly considered it, but decided against it after less than a minute of serious thought.

During his time spent in the service, Nolan had been taught the art of countersurveillance while attending a specialized school. However, he was particular about when and where he applied that practice. In times of war, or when overseas in a scary place like Beirut—or pretty much anywhere in the Middle East—it made perfect sense. When dealing with suspected terrorists or spies or other high-level professionals, it made sense as well. But when dealing with buttoned-down businessmen, arrogant executives, tech geeks—and he considered Johnny Blue to fall somewhere in the vicinity of one, if not all, of these lesser categories—then it was a total waste of time. And James Nolan did not like his time "o'wasted," especially on some rambling dude who would come and go faster than a blistering ass rash.

Eighteen

Johnny Blue was on a speaking circuit roll. He was booked solid eighteen months out and his popularity was increasing by the millisecond. He was preparing for a stadium speech at a West Coast university—an outdoor appearance where an expectant crowd estimated at twenty thousand was going to show. Not everyone attending would be there to see him, but he was the main attraction along with a half-dozen other speakers peddling their orated wares.

From a grassroots perspective Johnny was having a good run. Conversely, from a conventional outlook he was loathed by many, which also meant he was having a good run. The mainstream pucker factor was tightening at an all-time sucked-in clench. Over five million followers—and still growing—had rid their respective households of televisions and other related services.

The establishment media outlets, left-right-middle, don't like losing viewers in blocks of millions. The advertisers for those outlets don't like losing viewers, either. The corporate and political elite don't like it when their friends who control the coffers are at risk of losing anything, especially so when an unknown muckraker starts building a gallery of intelligent voters who are in complete control of choice—choice of content read, choice of content heard, choice of content viewed—and who have an acute awareness regarding personal action.

There was a fear of ideas in the air, and Johnny Blue was on fire touting pronounced truths. But what continued to piss off the glitterati, what continued to chap the mainstream media's hide, was Johnny's unwillingness to meet with—or go on the record with—them. And then there was Lawyer Bill, also a media nuisance, with his continuing elevated yowl of how inconsequential they'd become.

There was another factor at play, too. Legal protests were on the rise in America. Eco-terrorism was on the rise as well, to include several bombings at facilities housing animals where inhumane testing was taking place. And there were rumblings coming from the dark web suggesting possible attacks directed at elite power structures: mass media, Hollywood, tech giants, and other corporate and authoritative institutions.

Certain political and media milksops cunningly directed an ineffectual finger at Johnny Blue when the subject of civil unrest and domestic destruction arose, a subject matter that they conveniently brought up. And they did so in a mousey, roundabout way after putting on their best serious face for the cameras to zero in on. Once their fake scowls were captured (pause for effect, adjust when necessary), they would pose passive-aggressive "what if" questions—along with predetermined hypothetical scenarios—instead of coming out and saying what was really on their mind. In gagging lockstep, they would ask their presumed expert panelists the softest of softball questions; set, designed questions to assist with making prearranged meaningless points.

Lawyer Bill had anticipated this deceitful strategy and advised Johnny to counterpunch in front of tens of thousands of people inside a college football stadium where the event was being telecast to the world via the internet, where millions of planet Earth's citizens would be watching, listening, and coming to their own informed conclusions. And Johnny took heed that sound advice, using conventional tactics against the cowering establishment media and their political and corporate cronies.

However, unlike his detractors Johnny didn't hint at anything; but instead, chose to be a standup guy, and, through a steady stream of verbal jabs, struck hard while using exact words against exact people. He quoted the belittlers word for word, stating precisely what they'd said, revealing their ridiculous lies and manipulative methods that had been aired live on TV and then shared on the internet for the masses to see and hear on a continuous loop. The crowd loved it, cheering Johnny on for pointing out a discernable bullshit stratagem while telling the scrub media and their political and corporate confidantes to respectively go fuck themselves.

Johnny (once again and for the umpteenth time) vehemently pointed out his continued nonviolent approach; and, with verbal flare, expressed that he would never tell another human being how to go about their life in a falsely-free or autocratic society. The crowd went apeshit wild, standing and cheering the fact that they were hearing a fresh truth and not being spoken to as if they were toddlers.

With his best performance to date—viewed by millions worldwide—Johnny Blue became a global sensation. He was elevated to the next troposphere, and someone who could not be ignored.

Nineteen

Arrogance, layered on top of narcissistic tendencies, layered on top of a steep intelligence quotient, can cause immense problems when the one possessing this cocktail of traits gets smothered by ego. Point being, Nathan Blue was taken aback when three FBI agents suddenly walked into his office without knocking. At first not much was said, until they stood him up, spun him around, and slapped a pair of handcuffs on him. And as he was being told that he was under arrest for a series of financial crimes and then Mirandized, he emotionally caved, letting out a faint whimper before starting to cry—like when a child gets caught red-handed stealing candy from a jar.

When taken into custody and given the opportunity to make a phone call, most folks reach out to an attorney. Not Nathan Blue. He reached out to his older brother. And, luckily, luck was bestowed upon him, because Johnny answered his phone after several annoying rings. Johnny's cell was rarely turned on, unless, naturally, he was using it. And, this time in particular, he was, as he gave the best advice one could give to another person in the hairiest of hairy legal situations: "Do not say a single word to the Feds—or to anyone else for that matter—until my attorney contacts you." With that, they ended their call and Johnny contacted Lawyer Bill.

And he did so for two reasons:

1. To aid in his brother's defense (if at all possible)

2. To get ready for an onslaught of media exposure once the press figured out that Nathan—a soon to be media-convicted white-collar crook—was related to yours truly, as in they were siblings.

Lawyer Bill was routinely ready for surprises. Rarely was he caught off guard by the countless predicaments human beings were prone to find themselves in. So he calmly listened to what Johnny had to convey regarding his brother's legal situation before asking a few follow-up questions. Finally, he wrapped matters up by saying, "I'm on it. Relax. Get on with whatever it was you were doing. I'll take it from here." And after hanging up, each man independently smiled, ever enjoying the game of chess they were playing.

Nathan was being held in protective custody, to include around-the-clock monitoring, because of who his brother was and not because of any money the authorities were convinced he'd stolen. And as he sat on a thin, foam mattress staring at a concrete wall, he found himself battling fear more than anything else.

His chief struggle was fear of the unknown. Having never before set foot in any type of lockup facility, his mind—racing at a thousand miles per hour—was venturing over to those scary places that TV shows and movies like to take you to. Those violent places where orifices get violated and skin gets slashed.

Not to worry, because the Feds mainly sought publicity. Make no doubt about that blatant fact. However, they were not seeking negative publicity associated with something going wrong with the man they'd just locked up; like, say, Nathan dying—whether it be self-inflicted or unfriendly assisted—or getting physically assaulted in any which way possible. The publicity the Feds deliberately arranged angled toward the bad guy looking like a bad guy while they came across looking like professional, trusted, humble servants just doing their jobs (aw-shucks).

And even though the authorities in charge wanted no harm to come to Nathan, the assigned federal interrogators surely employed the likelihood of physical violence as an interrogation tool, as a scare tactic, especially when Nathan followed his brother's advice by keeping his mouth zipped shut until Lawyer Bill arrived. A silent suspect will undoubtedly receive a barrage of threatening innuendos—a bombardment of bluffs and rehearsed bullshit—from intimidating, seasoned interrogators who are used to the basic of all basic trickery getting the job done in most cases.

For Nathan, the worst part of incarceration was isolation. He was dumbfounded by the fact that even though he detested the presence of most human beings, when denied access to them, whether a rapport existed or not, it robbed him of something he couldn't quite describe. An emptiness. An incompleteness. And he felt a sense of pain related to that void. For sure an uncomfortability, and maybe, just maybe, a yearning. Whatever it was, it didn't feel right.

So, there he sat—sad, depressed, scared, yet also conniving. At the core of the matter, he was the only one who truly knew the sum of his dishonest deeds. He sensed that the federal agents sent to interrogate him were guessing, reaching, and definitely bluffing. They did not know how far back he had begun stealing company funds. He was sure of that. And if they didn't know "when it all began" then they definitely didn't know "how much was taken."

Nathan was also the only one who knew where all the money was stashed, in the many nooks and crannies located throughout the scarcely regulated banking world; a world where affluence freely roamed. Moreover, he was the only one who knew the numerical sequence of codes that rendered access and movement to millions, as in monies totaling eight figures and change. In recent times he had done a poor job at covering his tracks—getting lackadaisical in the last sixteen to eighteen months—but had done a full proof job of proper thievery the seven years prior to his sloppy ways.

With his mind working overtime, he was mulling over three important questions:

1. Can I trust Lawyer Bill?
2. What percentage of money am I willing to part with?
3. How much time am I willing to spend in federal prison?

Forty-eight hours later they were together, alone in an assumed-to-be-private, barebones room—Lawyer Bill and Brother Nathan—their first meeting in the flesh. Bill chose to call him Brother Nathan, so as not to forget why he was representing this high stakes thief.

If for a second Nathan thought Lawyer Bill was going to underestimate him like the Feds had done, well, then, he was going to be sadly mistaken. Bill had dealt with hardcore criminals his entire career, from day one after establishing a private law practice. Lawyer Bill didn't underestimate anybody, nor did he get caught up in perceived reputation or status. And he never judged clients based on appearance: a tatted up biker gang dealing guns and drugs, a nerdy explosives expert who could blow up a city block if agitated, or a well-to-do housewife who had dismembered her cheating husband in the guesthouse bathtub. For Bill, it was mostly about business.

Bill advised Brother Nathan to say as little as possible and, if necessary, to do so in hushed tones. This was not the counselor's first rodeo. He had with him a notepad and pen. Questions and answers were to be captured on the second page of the notepad, with the first page providing cover: write question, slide notepad over, read question, write answer, slide notepad back, acknowledge answer, repeat until finished.

Then, in a low whisper, Bill made his first official statement: "If you lie to me, or if I sense that you are lying to me, then I walk away. I'm not here for you. I'm here as a favor to your brother, and he's well aware of the conversation I'm having with you right now. Secondly, I'm very connected in the prison world, as in I know and do business with powerful men. I'm talking about men who are locked up for life, men who could prevent serious harm from coming your way, or, conversely, and in total enjoyment, allow horrendous things to happen to you. Either way, they control everything inside these prison walls. Do you understand completely—with no confusion whatsoever—what I just said to you?"

Nathan nodded his head up and down.

Bill said, "Good, let's get on with it."

"I will write the letter "Q" followed by a question. You will write the letter "A" followed by a brief answer. Do you understand?"

"Yes."

Q: How much money are we talking about?

A: 63

Q: MM?

A: Yes.

Q: What do they have on you that is provable?

A: 3.5MM in the last 18 months at the most.

Q: You're positive about this.

A: Yes. 100%.

Q: In your defense, can I muddy the waters by tying in company executives, partners, board members, confusing data and related paperwork?

A: Easily.

Q: In terms of funding, you control access to all locations?

A: Yes.

Bill spoke again, but also used pen and paper for full explanation. Pointing with pen at written figures: Me = 10MM. Your safety = 3MM. "We will eventually float the idea of payment back to your employer in a good faith gesture. We will subtract an additional 3.5MM to cover that for now, but we will never admit to or settle for that sum of money. Worst case scenario, moneywise, with government demands not included, I'd say you'll be left with somewhere in the neighborhood of 46.5MM. But let's be conservative in our thinking. Figure 45MM instead due to unknown obstacles. That would leave you with a little more than 70% of the original take (Bill had to show the thieving accountant that he, too, had a solid grasp on rudimentary numbers). But hear me out on this, I will be greatly surprised if at least one curveball isn't thrown your way during the legal shitshow you're about to go through.

"Now, in terms of your incarceration, again worst case scenario, I'd say five years in a minimum security federal prison. I think I can get that reduced to somewhere in the vicinity of 18 to 36 months. Maybe less, but probably not.

"And just so we're clear, I'm not open to financial negotiations on any of the terms previously mentioned. I make no promises and won't be offended if you don't want to do this deal. I'll walk away right now, no hard feelings. That said, are you willing to do this deal with me within the parameters discussed?"

"Yes."

Crossroads: "Now is when you write down instructions and codes for access to those accounts that cover the agreed upon amount. Now is when you put trust in someone you barely know. But I can guarantee your safety and a relatively short amount of time spent inside while only withdrawing 16.5 million and not a penny more unless the government demands more."

With that, Lawyer Bill placed an envelope on top of the notepad and slid it over to Nathan. There was a blank piece of paper inside. Bill's final words: "Write it all down on the paper inside the envelope. I'm quite familiar with handling international money transfers and the laws associated with them. Or, in this case, no laws. So, be exact. Make no mistakes. And once you're done, place the paper back inside the envelope and seal it."

Brother Nathan did what he was told to do. He had no other choice.

Twenty

It started off with a blast from a brass horn; from the adept chops of a known jazzman. Johnny Blue nearly burst out laughing because he'd been elevated to a level where musical riffs preceded introductions. Though thought to be funny—in his mind, anyway—he wasn't so sure it was necessary but would play along with the festivities. When in New Orleans, do what the folks in The Big Easy do.

Johnny was dealing with questions from a myriad of media engineered attacks, all attempting to ascertain snippets of information about his brother and his brother's troubles. He had put out a blanket statement at the request and design of Lawyer Bill, a straightforward declaration explaining his noninvolvement concerning Nathan's professional career and subsequent legal issues. But that was far from enough in the eyes of most news groups who wanted to connect the dots of illegal activity that had absolutely nothing to do with Johnny Blue. Nothing at all.

Lawyer Bill, in a not so elegant way, put the whole thing in perspective: "It's a silly game, Johnny. And today you're a big deal. But tomorrow, after yet another mass shooting or when another priest gets caught fucking more little boys, then that will be a big deal for half a minute and you'll be old news, my friend. Until then, we'll deal with the absurdity of it all. Fuck 'em, feed 'em fish."

Johnny laughed, an actual out loud laugh, after the seasoned trial lawyer expressed himself with such profound originality. It was a game. The overwhelming majority of sycophants—the bootlickers who all too often find themselves on their knees bent toward conformity—don't care about the truth.

What they care about is gossip, self-agendas, and personal look-good. What they really care about is self at the expense of losing self. The world had become a farce, a slapstick comedy that revolved around poor direction. Where were all the truth seekers?

And as he topped the stairs and headed for center stage, as he approached the mic stand, he stared out at an ocean of multicolored humanity, at people who had traveled long and far to hear a truth seeker speak because they, too, were truth seekers. Collectively, they were tired of the apparent charade. He spoke from the heart, as he was very much moved and overcome with emotion, overcome with loneliness and exhaustion and mental struggle.

And then it happened—feelings coupled with fatigue apexed. The crowd sensed his fervor and passion matched passion. They were one, with a clear understanding resonating throughout Fair Grounds Race Course.

He finished his speech with yet another challenge. By strategically piggybacking off the "trash your TVs" campaign momentum, he set aim on the banking industry—the new business sector in his crosshairs—and, more specifically, credit cards. Any and all credit cards.

Johnny had done the research, finding out that Americans possessing credit cards, possess, on average, 3.7 cards each. He rounded that number up to four and pushed his new agenda, his new campaign.

He informed the crowd—the largest he'd ever been in front of—about the four-card, credit card average. As a broad-brush example, he asked that they cancel three of their four cards, imploring them to get down to one- or none-card if at all financially feasible. And he voiced his goal: five million people times three cards each equals fifteen million credit card cancelations at the least.

"Let the banking industry feel your thunder!" shouted Johnny Blue.

That would definitely get the banking industry's attention. It would garner attention from many if realized. The crowd thought it to be a grand idea, as they cheered and roared for the man on stage.

Truth seekers united.

Twenty-one

Like a frightened jackrabbit, the "cancel your credit cards" campaign set in motion at a horse track in Louisiana took off in full stride. The original goal of fifteen million credit card cancelations was easily surpassed in less than ninety days. Holy shit!

The card cancelation numbers reached then exceeded the twenty-two million mark in a little over four months, with nineteen million cancelations taking place in the good ole US of A. Yikes! Whether Johnny Blue was ready for a fight or not, he had found one—as in put up your dukes—from the dirtiest of all dirty fighters, the unscrupulous side of America's government, plus a few wealthy folks yielding power thrown in for good measure.

Johnny was being torched by just about every media outlet that still had television play. Shunning hypocrisy, he only got wind of this scorching by word of mouth—in tiny increments of "did you hear this" or "did you hear that,"—from those who couldn't comprehend that he truly didn't care about the ne'er-do-wells who opine from tarnished pulpits at high-volumes of inanity. Paying little attention to mainstream anything, Johnny went about his business as usual. And then something strange happened.

While heading home from a speaking engagement and settling in at a campground in an unknown desert town on the New Mexico/Arizona border, two linebacker looking gentlemen paid him a visit. They wore cheap, dark suits and had official identification and everything, looking the part of who they were—government lackeys—with demeanors that were threatening in a one-stayed-quiet-and-stared while the other-dropped-menacing-hints sort of way.

Johnny simply let the talker talk and the gawker gawk. And when the talking was done, he handed over one of Lawyer Bill's business cards. After looking at the thick stock card, the talker, said, "Hiding behind a lawyer, eh?

Johnny's response, "Canadian, eh?" The big fella didn't quite get it. Wasted sarcasm. Too bad.

Even funnier, the two simpletons didn't know that Shakes, standing quietly by Johnny's side, was recording the whole thing with his helmet cam—audio included. Lawyer Bill was reviewing said video within fifteen minutes after it was captured, as he wrapped it up by watching the two beefy men's departure. And prior to that, when zooming in on the two government identification cards, he thanked his lucky stars that technology had advanced to such an elevated level in his lifetime. Then caution set in as he realized that this technology thing works both ways. With realizations hitting home, Bill concluded that Johnny would have a heightened level of security moving forward, plus two bodyguards accompanying him on all future road trips.

James Nolan sat and watched from inside a pop-up tent trailer, sixty yards away, grinning. An in-focus monocular covered his right eye. His grin stemmed from watching two FBI goons attempting to act like intimidators. Nolan thought, 'If you're going to pull a gun, then you better be prepared to use it. And if you're going to act tough, then rough somebody up, as in beat some serious ass to a bloody pulp. Anything else was simply amateur hour, a bad bluff during a game of chance while playing with pros.'

Johnny Blue had surprised even Nolan, who figured that the credit card stunt was the topper and probably the final straw. You can't go around putting the squeeze on the banking industry. Money doesn't like money taken away, regardless of methods used when removing those funds. That was a major faux pas on Mr. Blue's part, an error in judgement that was going to cost him plenty, going to cause him serious problems—attorney protected or not.

'Oh well,' thought Nolan, as he contemplated his orders and where things were heading. He'd get a good night's sleep and take off an hour after Johnny and company eased on down the road in the early morning. And then he thought, 'Thank God for small, magnetic GPS trackers, not that God had anything to do with it.'

Shakes chose to hang outside alone, chill'n outdoors and taking in the beautiful desert night—the space, the quiet, the unlimited stars. Much different than the city in which he resided. Quite an assortment of new things were taking place in his life, and he was enjoying every minute of it. He continued to shoot video up until nodding off into comfortable sleep.

Twenty-two

A deal had been struck with the government. A deal had been struck with Nathan's former employer, too. Nathan should have been feeling what the Twelve-step community refers to as "an attitude of gratitude," but he wasn't capable of fully grasping fundamental concepts laced in appreciation and kindness.

He had, however, concealed his thievery well, outsmarting the government financial experts as well as his former employer's top executives. Nathan was proficient at the pilfering side of his trade and had stumbled across a group of rich businessmen, fools really, who didn't have the proper checks and balances in place to determine how much damage had really been done. Not sure who said it first, but with Nathan Blue and his former business partners it certainly rang true: "There is no honor among thieves."

Lawyer Bill had presented the good news to Nathan in person, face to face. To borrow from the customer service industry, Lawyer Bill had "under promised and over delivered," at least on the sentencing side of things. Nathan was sentenced to an additional six-month stint in a minimum security federal prison. Having already spent nine months in lockup (which counted as time served), he was going to spend in total fifteen months behind bars. Not bad at all.

To get to this point, Nathan had agreed to give back two million dollars as reimbursement to his erstwhile employer. However, the government also demanded supplemental monies from Nathan for what they described as filing false tax returns as well as a host of other related financial misdeeds; in all, totaling an additional two million dollars. An overblown demand? Probably so, but sometimes—when naked and bent over a barrel—you have to pay to play.

And then there was the final financial bee sting, a painful stick that set Nathan off on an emotional rant. He would have to pony up yet another two million dollars on top of the four million dollars already earmarked for the Feds and his former employer. The add-on money was for his lawyer to secure personal protection at the new penitentiary he was about to be shipped off to for his final months in lockup.

Lawyer Bill had to convince Nathan to pay up, as in six million greenbacks that he hadn't planned on parting with but had certainly been warned about. Prior warning aside, Nathan pushed back, screaming that the government was ripping him off, that Lawyer Bill was ripping him off.

What Nathan didn't quite get, not completely, was that if he pulled his head out of his ass and played his cards right he was going to mosey away from federal prison as a multimillionaire, and, as a bachelor, because the trophy wife was gone, long gone, with child in tow. Once released from custody, he would be free to go wherever and do whatever he damn well pleased; for the most part, anyway.

Nathan stood to walkaway scot-free with 44 million tax-free American dollars, and well within range of the 45 million dollar mark Bill had guesstimated during their first attorney-client meeting. Not bad, indeed.

Without merit, Nathan accused Lawyer Bill and the government of financial exploitation, and he continued to voice this concern while mired in greed and self-pity. He was irate, because to meet his financial obligations he now had to give his attorney access to another one of his hidden bank accounts, an account of lesser value than the remaining untouched accounts. Bill sat back in an off-green government chair and looked across the table in complete disgust, staring down at the enraged accountant and saying nothing. Nathan eventually felt the heat and shut up.

After several seconds of silence, Bill calmly reminded Nathan that he still needed to stay alive for six more months—in a different penitentiary where protection came at a steep price—before he could go live a life of luxury in a country that did not have an extradition agreement with the United States. After swallowing hard and letting the counselor's remarks sink in, Nathan slowed his ungrateful roll and began writing down account access information on a piece of paper that Bill had slid his way. Too late, as Lawyer Bill thought, 'Highly intelligent white-collar criminals are often too smart for their own good. Which makes them not that smart at all.'

When Nathan first met Lawyer Bill he had nine offshore bank accounts stuffed with money stolen from his former employer. Initially, he gave Bill access to five of those nine accounts in an effort to cover newfound legal and personal protection costs. He now felt like he was bleeding money, as he was about to pay out more than originally anticipated. Easy come, but not easy go, with the first round of money soon to be gone. Five drained, four remained.

Nathan, in full-on poker face mode, in full-on fear mode, was silently conniving. He feared that his attorney was about to rip him off. Because if Bill cleaned out what little money was left in the original accounts—plus the funds from the new account—then he stood to walk away with even more of Nathan's pilfered money. In a bout of desperation, Nathan concluded that he needed to put himself in an advantageous position; a position where he could eventually eliminate Lawyer Bill.

 And then in complete contrast to his earlier temper tantrum, Nathan happily handed over the account access instructions, and said, "I'll tell you what, close out the original five accounts and do the same with the new account. After expenses you'll be left with eight million. Place those monies in a secure, safe place of your choosing and hold onto it until after I get out of Club Fed. I have complete trust in you. Are you good with that?"

 Pause.

 Lawyer Bill was faintly impressed at the calculator type speed that Nathan's brain computed numbers. However, the old-time counselor still had a pretty good handle on basic mathematics as well. Numbers aside, it made no sense whatsoever for Bill to watch over a portion of Nathan's money. In fact, he wanted in and out of those accounts as quickly and as few times as necessary—leaving the smallest of traceable digital footprint—which meant he only needed in and out one more time.

Bill looked into Nathan's eyes and knew right away that he was being set up. He sensed a high-tech trap looming. For the first time in Lawyer Bill's presence Nathan had earned a whit of respect. He'd also made a huge mistake.

Nathan erred when he said he had "complete trust" in Lawyer Bill. He had blundered badly right then and there. A big-time slip, and what they call a "deal-breaker" in the business world. Bill knew for a fact that Nathan didn't trust anyone, probably not even himself. 'Fuck empty words,' thought Bill, 'and fuck Nathan Blue,' as he smirked inside, not showing outward emotion but knowing without question that Nathan Blue was a sleazy, degenerate thief. A used car salesman lacking empathy, shame, or any sense of loyalty.

End pause.

Bill spoke, saying, "That won't be necessary. Like I told you the day we first met, I'll remove from your accounts only what's needed, and not a penny more."

With that, Bill stood and extended his right hand. Nathan, not sure what to do, stalled for a bit, then clumsily stood up and shook his lawyer's hand. Bill took a final look at the accountant, sizing him up, before they both peered deep into cold, saurian eyes.

Finally, he said, "Good luck," before turning around and knocking on the only door in the room. And as the jailer escorted Bill toward the exit point, he knew for certain that he would never see Nathan Blue again. It's the way he wanted it. It's the way they both wanted it.

Twenty-three

In wordless ease, Shakes and Johnny sped down the road. They were heading toward yet another speaking engagement and followed close behind by a bodyguard driving a two-door, eight-year-old, impeccably conditioned Audi A5. Destination: The high desert of Northern Nevada—a willing audience revved and waiting arrival. Johnny Blue had convinced his savvy attorney that one bodyguard would be sufficient, as long as "my guy" signs off on the right candidate. Johnny's wish was granted after a complete background search checked out on the poor soul rounding out his mismatched staff.

The bodyguard signoff process had been pared down to one uniquely qualified candidate; a "her," a Moira Montez, and not a "him," as assumed by Lawyer Bill and Johnny Blue, but never presumed by the curriculum vitae sorters, Zamora and Shakes, who'd been entrenched in the selection process from the very start. Rob completed all relevant checks from behind the scenes, from a distance and with trusted sources, while Shakes assisted as the lone middleman, the interviewer of the interviewees and the face to a name.

A limited number of people had knowledge of a distant relationship between Rob and Johnny, with but a handful clued in to a current alliance. Rob Zamora was Johnny Blue's hidden confidante. In the Blue camp, Rob's name was rarely bantered about and, if mentioned at all, only mentioned in whispered timbres in one-on-one settings. There was an unspoken understanding that if the shit hit the fan, then this silent mystery man would come to the rescue.

Outside Johnny's circle, odds favored that a small, select group of individuals actually knew Zamora. And as far as government concerns went, Rob hadn't used anyone from the Blue clan as a reference when enlisting in the military way back when. All references from back in the day were connected to former teachers, coaches, and employers; acquaintances, really. The type of people who would laud on and on about the first-rate attributes of a naïve teenager aspiring to join the Marine Corps. Reality was, only a few aged Nebraskans had bygone, murky memories of the Blue/Zamora duo running around together in their youth.

When traveling as a group or tandem over an extended period of time a certain etiquette needs to develop if relationships are to stay intact. Touring bands go through it, tightknit military units go through it, sports teams go through it, and, Shakes and Johnny Blue—like those previously mentioned—had to go through it.

In what should materialize quickly, involved parties fall into an unspoken understanding. And if assimilation isn't swift, then you can bet a fat month's paycheck that the relationship—the team, the band, the duo, the group—won't survive but short-term, let alone long-term. No way, no how.

I do this, you do that. We speak when we speak, we fall silent when we fall silent. And silence is key. The ability to be comfortable without words, without unnecessary chatter or electronic static. Tranquil inside a wordless cab with the meditative thrum of molded tread rotating over well-worn highway. Just you and your thoughts. The reading of an obscure billboard. The observation of an open field; a protective coyote watching from afar as you trek through her domain.

Shakes broke the silence by asking, "Why'd you get sober?" That's all it took to end hours of quietude. Johnny easily transitioned from stillness to spoken word—a story to tell, a perspective to share.

"The short version, I got sober because I needed to get sober. But let me tell you something, it's not that easy to rid oneself of an addiction. That's why they call it addiction, and it's a complicated, twisted mess with a mind of its own.

"I did drugs. I drank alcohol. But I loved alcohol. She was my mistress. I loved the way she made me feel. I loved what she did for me.

"To get off work, to temporarily withdraw from the rat race and walk inside a dingy bar—the pour, the anticipation—and to finally slam those first two shots of high octane booze on an empty stomach. Then the short wait, as the alcohol releases into your system and begins performing its magic.

"For me, there was nothing else like it. It's a feeling I can only compare to teetering on edge that split second before cumming. Pure joy. A chemically enhanced joy, but still joy just the same.

"Most people sitting in positions of judgement see what alcohol and drugs do to the addict. But what they're missing—what they don't entirely get—is the fucking point. And the point is this: What do the chemicals do for the addict? And if the answer is 'everything,' then I feel for the user, and, hold on, because it's going to be a long, rough ride, especially if they've stumbled across that one substance or combination of unique chemicals that their body loves, craves, and can't live without.

"Alcohol gave me confidence; however false it may have been. It helped me feel at ease in risky situations, made me comfortable staring down danger. It helped me talk to women, to be around them, to be with them. It assisted with bullshitting my bosses, my clients, whomever. It helped me climb the corporate ladder two steps at a time. It made me feel invincible, with little to no remorse the next day when coming to from oblivion.

"Alcohol became my identity, and it kept me warm and safe until it didn't. So, when alcohol was no longer my savior, when my mistress moved on, I became scared and lost and didn't know what to do. That's when the spiraling out of control began.

"And that period of spiraling down a dim, gray drain while still drinking and using was a two-year decline into the abyss. Then, and not to sound too dramatic, I had an epiphany in the middle of a forest up in Northern California and that pushed me to ask for much needed help, led me to where I'm at today.

"But even the getting help phase wasn't easy. It was the complete opposite of easy, with a bunch of insecurity thrown in for good measure. I checked myself into a 105-day outpatient rehab facility for people struggling with chemical dependency issues. I thought I wanted to be in rehab, I really did, until my first day there.

"Physically I was fat, with some minor liver problems. And mentally I was pissed off with an out of control ego. I had all the answers to all the questions. So I thought, anyway. The second day at the facility sucked big-time, too. But then, from out of nowhere, something happened, and it happened for me on day three. Something clicked, causing me to believe that I had to fully accept the recovery process, fully accept the steps to getting sober, or, it wasn't going to work out well for me. I approached it like my drinking: All in or why bother. I chose all in.

"On top of rehab, I also had to attend AA meetings—one, two, sometimes three, four, five meetings a day my first year of sobriety. I didn't have to go to that many, but I took it to an extreme level. Again, identical to my drinking. And by the time I finished rehab, I was surfing the 'pink cloud.' That's an AA term, and I can only describe it as 'being high on being sober.' It feels like a drug. In a sense, it is a drug. An emotional drug.

"But life moves on, and pretty soon you're navigating life as a sober person. And that's a scary place to be when you're emotionally raw and, at that exact same time, coming to the realization that you're starting fresh, anew, with everything: relationships, work, friends, family, whatever. Try having sober sex for the first time in twenty years. Talk about inhibitions.

"If you're lucky, and I mean really lucky, then you figure out that not everybody in your life is good for you, or there for you, or that they ever were. And maybe, just maybe, you're better off parting ways with cancerous ties. I call it the beginning of the decent from the 'pink cloud.' Actually, it's more like a crash-landing.

"Let me give you an example. True story: I'd just gotten out of rehab and I attended a family reunion. I was probably four months sober, if that. Most everyone there was aware that I'd recently completed a program, and, throughout the event, one or two people would come up and shake my hand or give me a hug and wish me well. They were truly happy for the changes I'd made. They gave a shit.

"At one point during the function I ended up in the kitchen with the spouse of a relative. Nobody else but us, and somebody I've known most of my life. She's at least twenty years my senior and someone you'd think would approach family matters from a position of support. I'd just gotten either a water or a soda out of the fridge and when I turned around there she was, just standing there looking at me. After a few seconds, she finally spoke, saying, 'I hear you're sober. We'll see how long this fad lasts.' Then, like a coward, she did an about-face and walked away, not wanting to stick around for the rebuttal, not wanting anyone else to witness her true self. Not that she was good at hiding it.

"But right at that moment, without hesitation, I knew. I finally knew exactly what she was: a resentful, misshapen ball of hate and cruelty. Reality was, I'd sensed that early on in life. As a kid. But with sobriety come affirmations—some pleasant, some not.

"Family dynamics are often tricky. And when the enormity of family is forced upon you as a child it can be daunting. It's not as if you get to choose your family. It's not like there's a selection process. Children are left with few choices, if any, as they're thrust into awkward encounters with the weird uncle; the creepy, untrustworthy cousin; the verbally abusive aunt; the violent dad; the excuse-ridden, codependent mother hiding from her past.

"You're taught to accept family like they're a trusted ally, as if the words "family" and "ally" are one and the same. How crazy is that thinking? Let's be honest, when you first meet somebody they're a stranger regardless of family ties or not. And this woman was bad for me, and bad for most people tangled in her wicked web. Truth was, most people simply tolerated her. But she was always bad for me— make no mistake about that—because I don't do well around deceptive cunts. Never have, never will.

"But the kicker was I wasn't mad about what she said. Not the slightest bit upset. I was simply presented with the truth. An ugly truth, but still the truth. And, luckily, I was absent feelings bent toward 'I'll show you.' To think that you have to prove something to somebody— whether they matter or not—is ridiculous. Because that's not what recovery is about. That's not what life is about. I got sober for me.

Nobody else. It was a selfish move. A survival move. I truly understood, and I still understand, that without sobriety I have nothing. Sobriety comes first. It's my newest mistress and has been for over a decade and a half.

"Here's the thing, miserable, unhappy people come and go, and they get seriously threatened when people around them change for the better. When others do what they can't bring themselves to do—take action, get help, shore up character flaws, admit truths— then the miserable dig in, as they hunker down in vats of their own shit while gushing vitriol. Misery does love company, and that is why the healthy, those seeking an honest way, ignore misery and misery's company.

"But what I left out of the story—and this is important—was that I locked eyes with her for a split second just before she turned around and walked away. That's right, we had an unspoken moment with no barriers between us. And I saw something as obvious as the nose on my face. I clearly saw a frightened, angry little girl. That's exactly what I saw. Then, in a flash, it hit me like a ton of bricks, as the truth welled up inside me in the form of a question. And I remember each word like it was yesterday, word for word, because those ten words are tattooed on the inside of my left forearm."

Johnny let go the steering wheel with his left hand and turned his arm at a slight angle so the words could be viewed in entirety. Shakes read slowly.

How many scars are inflicted by those scarred and affected?

The two men again sat in silence. After a beat, Johnny broke in by asking, "You want to stop and get something to eat?"

Shakes said, "Yeah, let's do that."

And they did.

Twenty-four

Moira Montez exited the freeway within four feet of the motorhome's bumper. Shakes had given her a heads up via text. She, too, was hungry and sent a return text: Glad we're stopping. I'm starving and I have to pee like a Russian racehorse. Shakes read her text twice—having never before heard that reference—and wasn't so sure he understood its meaning, but, at any rate, still laughed his ass off.

The two men waited as Montez cruised the perimeter of the diner's parking lot. After determining zero threats, she parked and went inside to scrutinize surroundings and effectuate safety precautions. Johnny felt uneasy about having a bodyguard, something Zamora told him he was going to feel. Rob also told him to let it go, saying that it was part of the deal but not a big deal.

Johnny reluctantly played along. Even so, he couldn't help but be impressed with Moira Montez—her thoroughness, her attention to detail, and the confidence with which she carried herself. She was not the type of person to fuck with, but definitely the type you'd want to work with. If Johnny had to have personal protection, then Montez and Zamora were who he wanted by his side, and maybe then they'd get to meet each other in the flesh.

After a stretch of time—ten, twelve minutes—she returned outside and scanned the parking lot, looking about and inhaling deeply a large dose of high-altitude air. Finally, she signaled the hungry travelers with a distinct nod. Time to eat.

Shakes went to the restroom while Johnny and Moira sat at a table for four; a table with chairs so as to avoid the trappings of a booth—one-way in, one-way out. Montez faced the front door while Johnny sat on her left. When done taking care of business, Shakes would sit on her right—a prearranged plan where none of their backs faced the main entrance/exit doors.

Johnny asked, "The wait outside seemed longer than usual, is everything okay?"

Moira looked up from her menu, and said, "It's all good. The delay was me. I had to pee so bad my lower molars were having boat races. That took up a little time. Speaking of which, don't you have to use the restroom?"

Johnny, contemplating boat races and floating teeth and trying not to laugh, said, "I'll take care of that before we leave. But thanks for asking."

Shakes made his way over to the table and, after sitting down, ordered eggs, bacon, and black coffee.

"Have you ever considered ordering something other than the usual?" Montez asked.

"Not from a dive like this," replied Shakes. Adding, "It's hard to fuck up eggs and bacon and black coffee. Plus, we have better food in the motorhome. I'm barbecuing bone-in ribeyes and asparagus tonight. You will not be disappointed."

Montez said, "Good to know. Looking forward to it." She then ordered eggs, bacon, and black coffee.

Johnny ordered the same.

James Nolan sat on a bed in a hotel room in Truckee, California, his laptop's battery life reading nineteen percent. Weary, he waited for an electronic signal—a beep, beep, beep, if you will—heading west on a return trip from Nevada. As he sat there, he thought, 'A high tech world may have made things faster and easier, but with technology comes boredom from waiting around for next, whatever next may be.' He was also tired of looking at porn.

Nolan was giving Johnny Blue and his cohorts free-range, plenty of room to go about their business while still keeping close tabs on their whereabouts, and easily gauging future locales by way of a posted online schedule. If anybody wanted to harm Johnny Blue it would not be difficult to pull off.

Nolan had done some snooping around to find out more about Johnny Blue's bodyguard. He was surprised that Johnny chose a woman for the role, but upon further review his astonishment diminished. And after learning a bit more about Moira Montez, he then asked himself a logical question: Who recruited her for the job?

The whole thing reeked of military or former military involvement. But the odd thing was, the known players involved had zero connections to the military and zero connections to government resources. Then he thought, 'Hell, these socialist fucks are all antigovernment.'

What then bothered Nolan more than anything was that his government connections had hit a roadblock when attempting a deeper dive into Montez's background. It appeared as if no one from her past knew that much about her besides what was already listed on her resume: military service, former employers, positions held, educational institutions attended, and certifications and degrees earned. The inability to dig extensively into her past was not a good sign, and he did not feel good about that Alaska-sized fact.

Nolan understood the Shakes connection. Johnny had found a tech-able kid in Silicon Valley's backyard who probably worked on the cheap and bought into Blue's ideological bullshit. However— upon second thought—how they met and how their work relationship unfolded was also a puzzling matter.

What at first appeared to be a simple assignment had suddenly turned complicated. Not crazy complicated but muddier than first assessed, like an unknown party was orchestrating specific deliverables from faraway wherever. Nolan wasn't worried, nor the least bit paranoid, but his cognitive senses were definitely heightened and he figured that to be a good thing.

Beep, beep, beep. Here comes next. He'd wait a while before following them at a safe distance back down the mountain.

Now in her thirties, Moira Montez was born and raised in Salinas, California. She was an only child reared by a Brazilian-Mexican-American father and an Irish-Scandinavian-American mother. She had a mix of blood that gave her a unique look; a look worth taking a second look—distinctive cheekbones, bright blue eyes, light brown skin, and an evenly proportioned body from head to toe and within an inch of the average height of an adult American male.

Moira's parents had died by the time she graduated from a two-year program at Monterey Peninsula College, where she walked away with an AS-T degree in mathematics. Her mother perished when she was thirteen after a head-on collision with a drunk driver. And her father passed during her first year of college due to complications related to prostate cancer.

After completing her two-year degree, she made the decision to enlist in the Army, saying to herself, "What the fuck, time to get out of California and see the world." So off she went to bootcamp in Columbia, South Carolina, followed by Army combat medic training in San Antonio, Texas. And shortly after that she was sent off to the Middle East to practice what she'd been taught, getting a whole bunch of on-the-job, in-your-face medic experience because of what happens to soldiers participating in war.

In the Middle East is where the junior medic met the almost retired Rob Zamora. That's right, she knew Zamora. They had actually met over a brief period of time. Regardless of how much time they'd spent together, she got to know him pretty well. Their little secret, and a relationship formed because of Jiu-jitsu.

Moira was an accomplished brown belt in a family line of Brazilian Jiu-jitsu practitioners. Rob Zamora was a wild grappler, with all moves learned stemming from his high school wrestling days. Lacking her grappling expertise, Rob was game to getting his ass handed to him by the Army medic when they were both stuck on base and bored to no end.

When presented with the opportunity, they rolled on a set of ancient grappling mats set on desert sand beneath a building's overhang. They rolled as often as possible. She taught Rob the basics of Jiu-jitsu, to include favoring technique over strength and the benefits of not giving up your back. And he soaked it up like a Portuguese sea sponge.

Moira had grown up under the tutelage of her father who had strong Brazilian Jiu-jitsu ties in both Rio de Janeiro and Monterey, California. She had competed in the art of Jiu-jitsu since youth and continued along the competition path through early adulthood. She often told Rob, "Technique and survival are key, but you are a strong, crazy motherfucker and I would hate to have to fight you in a dark alley down in Rio." To which Rob would reply, "If you shoot me first with a .45, you'll be just fine."

Like most military relationships—when reassigned, when retired out, or when dead—they end. It's part of the deal but not a big deal. However, when Moira answered her phone, she instantly remembered his voice and that matter of fact manner of speech. She smiled, thinking back to distant days when he used to utter, "Fuck me, not again," a second before tapping out to a rear naked choke.

Johnny Blue and crew returned to Reno in a borrowed pickup truck: newer, full-size, four-wheel drive. They had left the motorhome and Audi with a trusted associate—with the man who owned the pickup—at his professional garage where both vehicles were serviced, washed, and detailed while Johnny was speaking to forty thousand desert rats a long drive away out into the far reaches of Northern Nevada's high desert; without question, in the middle of dusty nowhere.

Johnny and Shakes retrieved their roller bags from the shop office and walked toward Virginia Street. The three were staying at a hotel for the night, in individual suites, four blocks down the road and paid for by a loyal supporter who respected what Johnny Blue was doing—to the extent that she began picking up the tab on Johnny and team's business related travel expenses. And they could thank Lawyer Bill for that.

Moira stayed behind with Jake O'Malley, the owner of the garage and the owner of an Irish pub—O'Malley's—that sat across the street less than twenty yards away. "Convenience at its best," was what O'Malley liked to say when pointing out proximity between businesses.

O'Malley was a retired Marine, a military mechanic by trade who'd flexed his entrepreneurial skills after leaving the service and returning to his hometown of Reno, Nevada. The town had changed quite a bit during his military absence. But gambling and alcohol and a decent car/truck/motorhome mechanic were still highly sought after in the Biggest Little City in the World. And if he liked and trusted you, he could assist with your high-tech needs as well.

Jake was of African American decent, and when the newfangled locals found out that he was the owner of O'Malley's, he would tell them that he was "Black Irish." They'd laugh—having no clue as to the term's meaning or origin—and then he'd set them up with another round of free drinks and watch as they fed twenty dollar bill after twenty dollar bill into any of the eight videopoker machines running side by side along the bartop at O'Malley's Irish Pub.

Moira and Jake crossed a narrow street. Jake unlocked the front door and they walked through the foyer and inside O'Malley's. Moira read quick a handwritten sign posted mid-upper door: Bar Closed. Private Event. She took a seat on a bar stool while Jake assumed his usual position behind the bar.

Jake closely resembled boxing's former middleweight champion of the world, Bernard Hopkins. And just like the former champ, he stayed in shape year-round and had a natural, unforced intimidating look about him. "What are you drinking?" Jake asked Moira. "Bourbon, water back," she replied.

He set her up with a generous shot of single barrel Kentucky bourbon and a glass of water while also pouring the same for himself. After taking a sip of whiskey, he handed her his cell phone, and said, "It's still there, undisturbed and in good working order."

Moira slid the phone's images along with her right index finger, occasionally pausing to look at the electronic contraption captured at a different angle from the previous pic. "I doubt I would've found it or known what it was if I did?" she said.

"It's state of the art," Jake pointed out. "It's well hidden and, from a technology standpoint, doesn't get any better than that; until, of course, some teenage tech genius invents a better one next week." To that, he chuckled while Montez adjusted in her seat and took a look around the bar.

O'Malley's was a tight rectangular bar with a dominant walnut bartop housing shiny videopoker machines several feet to the right of the foyer—the lights and bells and whistles that grabbed your attention upon entering. The bar was fully stocked, bottles resting on glass shelving and backed by a mirrored wall; reflective multi-colored liquids seducing guilty patrons. A single pool table took up most of the industrial concrete floor between the foyer and a lone hallway, with just enough room on all four sides to keep the fire marshal happy. The hallway led to two bathrooms and the back door. That was it.

Montez: Pretty efficient setup you have here.

O'Malley: I like keeping things simple. And clean. In Nevada, if you have a gambling license, and I do, you make your money on gambling. Booze takes a back seat. And, hopefully, the gamblers are shitty gamblers; which they usually are. I bring in fifteen to eighteen thousand a month off these poker machines alone. I'll give out a few free drinks, no problem, and then sit back and watch as someone feeds five hundred dollars into a machine over a couple of hours' time. Five, six drinks later, maybe—and I'm talking about a big fuck'n maybe—they win back eighty. They leave here with a slight buzz and think they did okay. I'm not a math major or anything, but I usually come out ahead on those transactions.

Montez: I am a math major and you do come out ahead, way ahead. So, where is this guy?

O'Malley: The man who attached the tracking device to Johnny Blue's motorhome?

Montez: Yeah, him.

O'Malley: He's currently in a hotel room on the California side waiting for you and yours to drive by so he can follow you back down the hill to Sacramento.

Montez: Do we fear this guy?

O'Malley: He is a professional killer with backing from a tiny department inside the United States government. So, yes, we fear him. But, he doesn't know what we know and he's a bit lazy. Check that. What he is, is complacent, and that's worse than lazy.

At the start, it appears as if he underestimated the situation at hand. However, he's not stupid, and I'm guessing he's thinking things through, like where exactly you came from. I say that because he's checked into your background. But he got nowhere because there's nowhere to get, and that has to make him wonder.

Also, he now knows that the motorhome never left Reno while you all made it out to the desert in another vehicle. Of course, you could have taken the Audi. But he should be thinking about where you stashed the motorhome during your time in the desert. Or, he's more complacent than I thought and doesn't give a shit.

Montez: So, where're we at with all this?

O'Malley: This is where we're at. Stick to the game plan. Keep on doing what we've been doing. Trust in Rob, he knows what he's doing and he's not complacent or lazy. It's all good, young lady.

Montez: I got your young lady swinging right here, old man.

O'Malley: Now don't go talking dirty to me, Montez.

Montez: Can I get another shot?

O'Malley: Absolutely. Good stuff, right?

Montez: Very good. Those Kentucky fucks make a mean bourbon.

O'Malley: Don't forget, they also play a mean fiddle and train fast racehorses.

Montez: Speaking of racehorses, mind if I use your restroom.

O'Malley: Don't mind at all.

Montez took a private elevator up to the floor below the top floor. As she walked down the hallway she spotted Shakes sitting outside his suite juggling a vape pen between hands.

Shakes: You want some smoke?

Montez: I only get high before I fuck.

Shakes just stared at her.

Montez: How old are you?

Shakes: I turn twenty next week.

Montez: The last time I fucked a teenager, I was a teenager.

Shakes just stared at her.

Montez: You're not the type of guy who falls in love after having sex are you?

Shakes: Hasn't happened yet.

Montez: You do know that I'm all-sexual, right?

Shakes: I didn't know that because I don't know what that means.

Montez: It means that I fuck who I want to fuck when I'm ready to fuck as long as they want to fuck.

Shakes: Got it. Have you been drinking?

Montez: I have. So, you want to get high?

Shakes: I do.

Montez: Then follow me, but don't fall in love.

Shakes, with vape pen in hand, jumped to his feet and followed her down the hall, before saying, "I promise, I won't fall in love."

Montez: Shut up, little boy.

Shakes grinned, and asked, "Should I go get a condom?"

Montez: Grab three and hurry up.

Twenty-five

Johnny Blue needed a break, and after a speaking engagement in Sacramento he would get just that: three weeks off with zero commitments. They drove from Reno to California's capital city in less than two hours, no stopping, not much talking. They again chose hotel lodging, a lesser hotel than the one in Reno but a hotel nonetheless, with running water and a bed and a toilet and a shower and much needed solitude. Oh, the comforts of life on the road when temporarily alone.

Johnny was sick of his own voice, tired of listening to himself speak. With that said, he was going to unveil his third campaign in Sacramento, a campaign centered around clean water and the overuse of plastic. 'Time to change things up,' he thought, 'time to reenergize.'

His mood was of a serious nature as he and Shakes and Moira approached the minor league park in her silver Audi; a ballpark named after a local retailer. Knowing that he was on the verge of facing much needed downtime gave him a boost of energy. He was gonna let it all hang out at this event.

He sensed good vibes within the intimate ballpark; only a few thousand people looking on. Easily eyeing the farthest reach of audience and not remembering the last time he'd been able to do that, he found an internal comfort, a calming of sorts. And after taking a deep breath, Johnny Blue let flow his truth.

In closing, he lifted an empty plastic bottle high above his head, and said, "Fuck plastic and fuck overpaying for water." The crowd sensed a change in tone, a definite urgency. Johnny preached on, "It's a sad day when Big Business coffers swell after giving corporate pimps the right to sell the people's water back to the very same people they stole it from in the first place; and to then do so in plastic bottles where carcinogen-laced biproducts end up in our bodies, end up in defenseless animals' bodies. That's not okay."

Johnny raised his voice: "A certain percentage of our populace have trace elements of plastic flowing through their bloodstream because we've been bamboozled into thinking that bottled water was a good idea. Fooled we were by that same corporate/political monster that at first said smoking cigarettes would not harm our lungs; that consuming margarine would not damage our arteries; that putting an overabundance of sugar in processed food was a grand idea and that it wouldn't cause ill effects on our blood sugar levels or raise the diabetes rates to an all-time nationwide high in adults and children.

"When I was a child there were plenty of public drinking fountains dispensing fresh, clean water. Tap water from our homes was safe and clean. Water from our garden hoses was safe and clean. It wasn't free, but the attached price for that water, whether in the form of utility bills or tax dollars, was reasonable enough and easily managed by the working class. Ask the fine people of Flint, Michigan, the following questions: How safe is your drinking water? And, who is taking responsibility—who is being held accountable—for poisoning your water and poisoning you and your children?

"The kicker: The typical markup on bottled water when compared to the cost of tap water is 280,000 percent. Let me repeat that: 280,000 percent. We should be rioting in the streets over such an abhorrent raping. Moreover, those plastic water bottles along with plastic everything imaginable are ending up in our oceans because the corporate businesses that we trust with our recyclable waste—that we pay to manage that waste—do us a disservice by recycling but a small percentage of that synthetic material. What they don't tell you is that they sell most of it to other countries who in turn profit from it before dumping the remaining unsellable waste into our oceans.

"From this day forward, never buy bottled water again. Quit using plastic bags. Avoid plastic altogether if at all possible. If need be, fill a metal container with water, those same containers that past generations referred to as canteens. Canteens and waterskins are not a new concept. They were our personal water carriers before plastic was created in 1898, before a cheaper, fully synthetic version was invented in 1907, and before this chemically manufactured ogre became widely produced and forced upon us in the 1960s.

"Look around the world today, into the isolated corners of nature—our lakes, our forests, our deserts, our oceans—and, odds are, you will find obvious evidence of unnatural debris in the form of plastic litter. Plastic has morphed into widespread lesions on Planet Earth's body. We cannot sit back and do nothing."

The crowd listened intently, understanding the severity of Johnny Blue's words—knowing that a factcheck would prove consistent with those words—as they came to grips with 280,000 percent markups and being sold something in a plastic container that should be reasonably priced and well conserved with the utmost integrity: our lifeblood—water.

In the end, Johnny Blue paraphrased words once spoken by George Carlin: *After human beings completely wipe themselves from this planet, Mother Earth will be just fine.*

Johnny Blue added a final take: "She'll recover in time having rid herself of the human parasite."

As he left the stage there was applause and cheering, yet an unspoken somberness filled the air.

Twenty-six

Shakes and Moira sat side by side on a bench inside The Mad Azorean. Immersed in thought, Shakes drank his usual cup of coffee with two add shots of espresso while Moira, content as a nursing baby, sipped at a drink from a frosty mug aptly named—in Portuguese—a Machado Baguncado: everything organic, where small-batch, coarse-ground Brazilian coffee is soaked for a minimum of twenty-four hours in artesian water sourced from New Zealand, then double filtered (paper followed by wool) before being bottled and chilled for another twenty-four hours; and, after much anticipation, poured over heavy Sonoma County grown whipped cream and topped off with a French Canadian maple syrup drizzle—a United Nations cup o' Joe experience not soon to be forgotten, and a tad bit messy to boot.

They were waiting for Johnny. All three wanted out of the city. All three were struggling with boredom of self while immersed in time off.

The problem with taking time off when you're used to being on the go is that you don't know what to do with yourself after a few days detached from the grind. And, make no bones about it, that's what Johnny, Shakes and Moira were battling. They were bored out of their collective minds. Minds that would not shut off. Minds desperately missing a prescribed pace.

Johnny Blue had a plan. And all three agreed to that plan. So there they were together again, as they walked out of the coffeeshop, jumped into his motorhome, and headed up to Bodega Bay for a five-day retreat away from San Francisco proper. To be as close to the water as possible.

Johnny rented a house on the bay—a big house with a private bed and bath for each. Inside was a fully stocked fridge. And outside, plenty of nature to walk around in with or without company. It gave them time to vegetate in private, time to talk business or nonbusiness, time to embellish first-time-shared stories, and time to eat home-cooked meals like a family might do. But most important, the Bodega Bay retreat provided well-earned rest and a true recharging while lounging amongst familiarity.

When the bomb exploded it did more than intended. A waste management facility in Tucson, Arizona, had been blown to smithereens. The unknown person or persons who'd pulled off the large explosion had hoped for a long-term shutdown of the profitable business, and to that they had accomplished their goal.

What they hadn't planned on (for damn sure) was killing two innocent people—two vagrants who had snuck onto the property after closing to wade through rubbish and hopefully find a prize. Instead, they found their demise.

The bomb investigators arrived at an all too obvious conclusion, stating that whoever made the bomb and subsequently detonated it knew what they were doing. And the establishment media's fat fingers along with scores of digits affixed to the hands of spineless politicians were now aimed directly at Johnny Blue. It appeared as if a limited number of words had finally caught up with him.

Every major news agency was showing a video clip of Johnny's most recent speech in Sacramento, focusing on the part about waste management facilities not holding up their end of the bargain. They purposely excluded his antiviolence rhetoric, but selectively left in the part about "not telling other people how to conduct themselves"—before mendaciously adding—"when going about their anarchist ways."

Trying their best to appear caring, TV media hosts put on yet another face—this time a sad face. Then, in hushed timbres, they employed their best sad voice when speaking about the two dead homeless people; two people whose names they could not remember or pronounce correctly if not for the syllable by syllable guidance enunciated into their earpiece.

Lawyer Bill referred to it as "a cherrypicked fucking over." The old-time counselor wasn't fazed in the least, appearing on the three major cable news networks as well as the local public station. He returned fire like an accomplished pro, hitting them head-on, pointing out that subversive groups—groups working against Johnny Blue—may very well have pulled off the Tucson bombing. "Hell, it could have been the United States government for all we know." Finishing with, "Apparently that's all it takes to get an ignorant reaction from the talking heads and their political pals who predictably follow suit."

Earlier, he had asked Johnny Blue, "Did you blow up that facility?" Already knowing the answer to the question posed, he made the point that, "Whoever set the bomb off was responsible for the carnage, and your words from a past event had nothing to do with it." Johnny found solace in the counselors remarks. Bill was right. Ignore the mainstream media and ignore the holier-than-thou politicians.

Johnny was readying himself for a small event in Pismo Beach, California. It would be a warm-up for an upcoming engagement in San Francisco's Union Square two weeks out. An outdoor event in the middle of the city. An event he'd been building up to. An event that was going to be broadcast worldwide.

To Johnny's surprise, the explosion in Tucson did not tarnish his fresh water/anti-plastic campaign. Reasonable people understood that a single person was not responsible for society's complete dysfunction. And with that, bottled water sales around the globe were about to dip while the elite guild spun in an erratic whirl because of one man's words, ideas, and popularity.

Congressional politicians were being inundated with phone calls and emails regarding safe, fresh water and the price associated with it. Protests were springing up in major cities, in the suburbs, in rural areas. Craven politicians had to be very careful when speaking about a man they detested, fearing reprisal from constituents who had a fondness for Mr. Blue. Those very same voters possessing the ability to think on their own.

With fingers crossed, the politically powerful and their corporate backers wanted Johnny to verbally dial it down a notch.

Then and only then could he take full financial advantage of his ascending fame.

They incorrectly assumed that Johnny Blue desired their compromised lifestyle.

Twenty-seven

The sniper takes special care when cleaning his precision rifle. He treats it like the expensive piece of killing equipment that it is, inherently understanding the respect it deserves. He routinely cleans it whether it needs it or not. When in doubt, break it down, clean it, and put it back together again—not taking better care of anything else in life.

At his request, Moira began to teach Shakes the art of Brazilian Jiu-jitsu. He already had a fundamental white belt ability from teenage days past but hadn't put in enough time or concentrated effort to advance beyond beginner level. Regardless, she started him off at square one and was somewhat surprised by his grappling attributes even though she'd felt his hardiness the few times they'd fooled around. Moira found herself inspired by Shakes' willingness—his humbleness, his attitude—to learn and to trust instruction. And Shakes was crystal clear about Montez's golden rule: If I'm going to be your Jiu-jitsu instructor then we no longer fuck. Understood? Understood. Good, so no popping a boner when I'm in the process of dislocating your shoulder.

Johnny Blue parked the motorhome at sand's edge, at an RV park a stone's throw from the Pacific Ocean and within lazy walking distance of the Pismo Beach pier. He looked out at a robust coastline; a low-populated jewel, particularly when compared to the state's ocean fronts in close proximity to major metropolitan areas. Not knowing the next time he'd have the opportunity to gaze out at an unpeopled beach, Johnny donned a pair of trunks and walked straight toward ocean waves, with the closest breakers peaking at two feet—two feet high and growing.

Twenty-eight

At his lawyer's insistence, Johnny made mention the Tucson bombing at the very beginning of his speech; not to belabor a point but to emphasize what foolery the establishment media was caught up in. He quickly moved on, saying, "Political hacks aside, why would any sane person tune in to watch news programs where the news anchors are forced to cover what their corporate advertisers tell them to cover? And what they speak to depends on what's selling that day—from both a news and product perspective—and which specific demographic can be lured in by shiny, artificial bait. Just because a stranger from TV-land tells us it's news, doesn't make it complete news or the whole truth. It is our responsibility to educate ourselves on facts and truths that exist outside conventional media hyperbole, and to call 'bullshit' when 'bullshit' needs to be called."

Next, Johnny gave an update on the campaigns he was pushing—TV abandonment, credit card cancelations, the fresh water/plastic trash dilemma—sharing recent statistical progress with the packed room that barely held two hundred people. He spent a few minutes on each campaign before tying them together with the obvious of all obvious points: "Why do the people not get what the people need, yet passively accept what Big Business and corrupt politicians say we need? As if they know. You would think that at this time in our history, in this country, of all places, we'd be much more aggressive with our actions when dealing with a deceitful power base. A power base that only benefits power and wealth and not the people."

Afterward, Johnny took questions from all-comers—not at all concerned with who they were or what media outlet they represented, if any. That took up another hour's time as he handled predictable questions like a pro while easily sidestepping verbal traps, fully understanding that certain media outlets were going to report what they wanted to report regardless of answers given. The last questioned was finally shouted his way.

Q: Even though you speak to personal nonviolent action, don't you find yourself complicit in the Tucson bombing by not condemning all violence?

A: No. Because violent action is not uncommon when the stakes are high. Think about all the wars that have been fought and are being fought across this planet as we speak. Show me a time in our history where that wasn't the case. If anything, history shows us that violent action is sometimes necessary, whether I agree with it or not.

As they drove back to the motorhome, Moira asked Johnny if he wanted to go home or stay one more night on the central coast. They elected to stay one more night—not a single one of them even semi-thrilled about a long drive home late in the evening.

Johnny Blue walked into the ocean first thing upon awakening, daring his cohorts to join him. A saltwater bath without soap or shampoo or a hot water valve, an eye opener and nipple hardener for sure. Moira called Shakes a pussy as she sprinted by; running, wading, then diving headfirst into an oncoming wave. Shakes was right behind her after peeling off his sweatshirt and tossing it on wet, packed sand.

Lawyer Bill was wrapping up final arrangements regarding Johnny's upcoming appearance in Union Square. He had met with event coordinators, police department representatives, a variety of media outlets, and other city personnel involved in the upcoming circus. The San Francisco Police Department had a recent history of managing such events with care and decency, with a certain professional etiquette. They'd improved on such things after incorrectly handling distant, past events that turned into near or actual riots because of overaggressive policing. Like anyone or any institution—when the opportunity presents itself—it's wise to fess up to wrongdoings while learning from past mistakes.

Twenty-nine

The gravedigger checks the grave monthly. After nudging the bulky steel a foot or two in one direction with the same tractor used to dig the grave, the gravedigger, on all fours, peaks inside to make sure it's an empty grave. It is.

The gravedigger sticks to the same routine every time: lowering self into grave—one hand on metal, one hand on dirt—landing, standing, kneeling, sitting down on bare earth. Slightly cold. Definitely damp. Dark inside but for slivers of light penetrating minimal space.

After lying down, the gravedigger contemplates surroundings, contemplates life—past, present—contemplates pending plans. The gravedigger smiles then laughs, not wanting to be too serious at this stage in the game. No, it's not a game. Not a dress rehearsal, but in fact real life. It's not, however, time to be serious. Not yet.

The gravedigger takes a nap, feeling comfortable in earth's safe room. Upon awakening the gravedigger listens to nature. Birds, squirrels, the rustling of forest inhabitants. Sitting up. Then kneeling. Finally standing. One hand on dirt, one hand on metal. The reverse from an hour ago.

Once the hunk of metal is pushed back in place, the gravedigger reworks groundcover. Checks the marker. Replaces it with another if missing or if it needs replacing—weather damaged or weathered away or simply the want of replacing.

Looks around. Back on the tractor. Leaving the forest.

Thirty

Nathan Blue had befriended a prison guard, a guard who chose the wrong profession, a guard who was easily steered by practiced criminals. With ulterior motives abound, Nathan convinced the balding guard to smuggle in a high-end, fresh off the shelf, brand spanking new smartphone. In return, Nathan would transfer the price of the new phone (fifteen hundred bucks and change) plus an additional 25K into an exclusive bank account where only the guard could gain access; not entirely true but facts weren't necessary when closing the deal. His final selling point was that once he possessed the phone, once he'd taken care of a few sensitive matters in private—man and phone alone—he would gladly give the guard a detailed tutorial on how to access his new account with a balance equaling near half a year's net income.

Nathan showed a level of patience that surprised even him, as he answered question after question after stupid fucking question repeatedly asked by the gullible guard. Finally the guard settled down, with happy thoughts prevailing as he contemplated spending his tax free take. It was a Tuesday, with the guard's scheduled off days on Wednesday and Thursday, which meant Friday would be the day that Nathan received his prize.

Since initial incarceration when his freedom was snatched away, Nathan was on the verge of possessing an unmonitored phone along with internet connectivity at his fingertips. First things first, he would link into several offshore bank computers and monitor personal account balances, with an emphasis on one account in particular. Trust was not one of Nathan Blue's stronger qualities.

He was feeling pretty good about himself once the guard let him be. Nathan had exploited another human being, another system, and would soon have the ability to see what his lawyer out in San

Francisco was really up to, to see if he put his trust in the wrong man. He surmised that Lawyer Bill was nothing more than a swindler and a seasoned con artist. Takes one to know one.

With the exception of nightly lockdowns in cramped quarters, Nathan Blue was feeling like his old self, a personal self he was enamored with—a conniving, selfish piece of work. And those self-absorbed thoughts aided his surging erection, as he turned his back to the cell door.

With cock in hand, he thought about his ex-wife stroking his hardness, her petite hands, her French manicured nails. He thought about what a scheming, conniving cunt she was—still is. He thought about how he could get her to do anything for money, anything, anything, as his heart rate sped like he was running uphill. And then his toes curled tight on prison issued flip-flops as he unloaded into a disposable cup.

Thirty-one

At first glance he appeared to be an elderly executive. He was slight in stature but not small, with salt and peppered hair. Perfect hair. Perfect length. Perfect fit to head. He had that. He also had a year-round tan and beautiful skin. A genetic gift.

He was in for life, in for more than life, which he thought to be absurd sentencing. From inside his boardroom he controlled just about everything, with juice extending beyond razor-wired fences. And but for Lawyer Bill and a group of sullied politicians, he would be in a maximum security prison and probably on death row—if not already dead.

They called him Mr. Eddie. And unbeknownst to Nathan Blue, the two would soon meet. Nathan hadn't paid him a whit of attention the countless times they'd shared the prison cafeteria—not once sitting close to the remote corner table where only a few trusted men were permitted to sit. Nathan Blue was clueless as to prison hierarchy, as to who Mr. Eddie was, because he had no interest in any of his incarcerated brethren. Throughout his life he'd suppressed an awareness tied to worldly ways and most other human beings; for his main interest lie with money and how to accumulate large sums quickly.

Mr. Eddie knew more about Nathan Blue than Nathan Blue knew about Nathan Blue; like, for instance, his breaking point. His primary survival instinct was to know who he was dealing with before actually dealing with them. He studied people. It's what he did. And he was not fond of surprises or unwanted attention. He was a calculated man who understood human tendencies—good and bad.

He was also a feared crime boss who'd had a long, successful run leading a crime organization in the Midwest based out of Kansas City. However, he was a dying breed who would die in prison. It was the hand he'd been dealt, and he would play out that hand to the very end.

Nathan was in heaven, by himself, a computer resting in the palm of his hand. The guard held up his end of the bargain, as did Nathan—making payment like he said he would. That didn't sit well with him, though, it would surely fester, because at his core he wanted to rip the guard off, steal from that loser and leave him with nothing. And if ever the opportunity arose, he would do just that.

After staring at the same number for far too long, Nathan cracked the smallest of smiles. He was actually surprised in a good way as his expectations weren't met. All of his money was intact. The San Francisco lawyer had not taken a cent of his remaining wealth. Not a cent.

And the sharing of passcodes was now past tense because relevant codes had been changed. Nathan was now the lone soul possessing confidential characters related to account entry. He grinned and thought, 'Fuck everybody. Who's the smart one? I am.'

Then, unexpectedly, there were three loud knocks on his cell door. Having been lost in thought, he was suddenly startled. Panic set in. Where to hide the phone?

He concealed the phone underneath a fetish based smut mag and quickly readied himself for company. The door eased open and two large guards he didn't recognize entered. Nathan looked up as one of the guards looked down, and said, "The boss wants to speak with you. Right now. And, before I forget, you need to bring the iPhone."

Nathan, trying his best to think of something to say, couldn't formulate a reasonable response, a reasonable lie. All of a sudden he felt as if he needed to use the bathroom. Damn it. The same guard spoke again, saying, "It's okay. We're gonna let you keep the phone. We're not interested in taking it away from you. But let's go, the bossman doesn't like waiting around for anybody."

With anxieties lessened, Nathan was led through a series of doors that were opened on command once the lead guard murmured jailer-jargon into a mic attached to his lapel. He was then guided through a maze of hallways and vestibules that he did not know existed, as he thought, 'How big is this place and why does the warden want to speak with me?'

After walking down a flight of stairs, they traveled through a well-lighted corridor before arriving at what appeared to be an office door. The lead guard knocked three times. And once commanded to "Come in," he opened the door and walked inside. Nathan followed close behind, wondering, 'Why does the warden have a basement office?'

At first glance Nathan was confused, with a series of questions coming to mind. But then he was ushered—more like picked up and moved—over to a classroom desk positioned in the middle of a large concrete room; an arm desk with left side entry where the occupant's right arm rests on an upside down and backward L-shaped desktop. There was one other chair in the room.

There Nathan sat, staring at a distinguished looking gentleman sitting in a brown leather chair with a monster of a man standing to his right—a man who was much bigger than the two large guards. Both men were wearing prison garb. But unlike any other inmate, their outfits appeared to be new and freshly pressed.

Nathan's right forearm was quickly duct taped to the armrest as if the tapers—the two guards—were working a pit stop at a NASCAR event. They had done this sort of thing before. The smartphone was placed on the desk.

The older gentleman, Mr. Eddie, spoke first, asking, "You are lefthanded, correct?"

Nathan, not expecting that question, said, "Yes," before asking, "Who are you and why am I here?"

"I'm Mr. Eddie, and you are here for two reasons. First, you are here because of a recent violation that apparently escapes you. I will explain that to you later, in detail. Second, you are here to take part in several money transfers. And if everything goes according to plan, you should walk out of here alive. Probably a little banged up, maybe missing a few parts, but alive. And walking out of here alive should be your main concern, son."

Nathan attempted to act tough. Not a wise move. But he tried anyway.

"First off, old man, I'm not your son and I don't think you know who I am. Also, remove this tape and let me go right this second or you and your friends here are going to be in big trouble with the powers to be within this institution; not to mention the serious blowback you'll soon be receiving from my attorney."

Mr. Eddie said nothing. Instead, he nodded at the goon standing by his side, who, without delay, walked over to the desk.

After approaching Nathan, he slapped him hard upside the head. Nathan had not been hit since childhood—in a playground altercation in elementary school. But in his adult life he had never been hit, not once, let alone slapped as hard as he'd just been slapped—like being struck with a two-by-four and not the palm of another man's hand.

Suddenly Nathan was disoriented, the left side of his head ached, it throbbed, and there was a loud ringing in his ears. He had spotty vision in his left eye and he felt nauseous. One of the guards removed the smartphone from the desktop, thinking that Nathan might puke. Which, a few seconds later, he did. Right in his own lap.

Mr. Eddie waited. When working, if warranted, he usually exercised patience. And as Nathan slowly regained composure, Mr. Eddie waited and then waited some more, waiting until Nathan had his wits about him before resuming their conversation.

"You do realize this is a serious situation, right?"

Nathan said, "Yes."

"Good," replied Mr. Eddie. Adding, "So here's the thing. You are going to transfer three of your four remaining offshore account balances in full over to a series of accounts that one of my associates will soon be sharing with you. Do you understand?"

Nathan, tonguing loose teeth and completely misreading the situation, abruptly blurted out, "I would never do that. I'd die first."

"That can be easily arranged," replied Mr. Eddie, as he again nodded at the goon.

Attached underneath Nathan's chair was a metal bookrack—just like in school. And on that rack sat a tool bag. The goon picked up the tool bag, unzipped it, and removed a pair of needle-nose pliers before setting the bag onto concrete floor. One of the guards, now kneeling behind the desk, wrapped his arms around Nathan's torso and held him tight against the back of the chair.

The goon, with pliers in hand, clasped the tip of one of Nathan's fingernails—his right pinky fingernail. Then, without precision or style, abruptly yanked the fingernail completely out. Nathan jerked and screamed as if surprised, then pissed and shit himself after experiencing the worst pain of his life. The guard held firm the bearhug.

Eventually Nathan settled down. And eventually the guard let go his hold.

Mr. Eddie, cool as a cucumber, then asked, "Are you ready to get on with the business at hand, or would you rather be taken apart piece by piece?"

Nathan, sweating profusely as he came to grips with the subsiding pain, said, "Let's get on with it."

Mr. Eddie continued, "Smart choice. Now let's transfer those funds. But first, let me tell you the good news. You'll be allowed to keep all the money in one of the heavier accounts. As you know, that's twelve million dollars. I'm sure that disappoints you. But let me be frank, I wanted to take it all. Your attorney, however, talked me out of it. Unlike me, he's a reasonable man.

"So, like I said, you get to keep twelve. On top of that, we're going to set you up with a new identity—a fresh passport with all the trimmings and citizenship in one of two countries that refuse to recognize extradition treaties with the United States. One country is in Asia and the other one is in South America. You have more than enough time to choose between the two. Once you've made that decision, let me know and I'll arrange all the particulars. Any questions?"

Nathan, defeated and feeling the sting of betrayal, said, "No. I don't have any questions."

Mr. Eddie nodded at one of the guards. The guard walked over to the door and opened it. In walked a woman in a well-fitted silk business suit sans panty lines; a leather satchel slung loose over one shoulder; a padded folding chair tucked tight under her other arm.

After setting the chair up within three feet of Nathan, she sat down, unzipped the satchel and removed a laptop.

She powered up the computer and waited a short while. Nathan, a disheveled mess—soiled and reeking—looked her up and down. She was dark-complected and of mixed descent, petite and athletically structured. She was braless, with barely a breast. She oozed confidence and was smart as a whip. She was a professional.

His sexual gaze was interrupted when she said something to one of the guards. Without hesitating, the guard approached Nathan and handed him back his iPhone.

She spoke to Nathan in a deep-timbred voice. "In exact order given, dial into each bank account and transfer all funds to the location code and account number that I'll be reciting to you prior to each transaction. We will begin with the smallest account first, the one holding the eight million—less twenty-six thousand five hundred eighty dollars and forty-nine cents as of this morning.

"If you think you are smarter than me and decide to deviate from my instructions, then you will lose a finger each time you decide to do so. If we get to a point where your right hand is without digits, we will then remove your testicles. After your balls, we'll remove one of your eyes. And we will medically keep you alive throughout the entire dismembering process."

With that said, she looked to her left. Nathan followed her almond shaped eyes that led to the man responsible for inflicting pain. He stood there staring, just staring—sadistically—like he wanted to fuck Nathan with the custom-made hunting knife in his right hand.

She asked, "Do you understand?"

Nathan said, "Yes."

She said, "Good. Because if you follow my instructions to a T, then I will show up at your cell one night in the not too distant future—after you've showered and cleaned up, of course. And on that night, you can fuck me any which way you want to fuck me. Any hole. All holes. Your call. And I will do those nasty things to you that your wife used to do to you before you found yourself locked up in a cage. Now, let's get on with it."

Nathan—still in pain, yet getting hard—said, "Okay."

Everything went according to plan; Mr. Eddie's plan. Relevant monies had been transferred, and, in the end, Nathan surrendered the final passcode to the sole account containing his remaining wealth. Mr. Eddie held Nathan's entire life—his financial and overall wellbeing—in the palm of his hand. And when his shiny iPhone was stomped into concrete until unrecognizable, until becoming synthetic dust, Nathan fully understood that he wouldn't do anything out of the ordinary without first consulting Mr. Eddie.

Once the guards left the room—ushering Nathan to the infirmary for minor repairs—the goon reached into his back pants pocket and pulled out a fresh pack of Nat Sherman Black & Gold cigarettes. He handed the pack of smokes to Mr. Eddie, before saying, "I really thought he'd hold out until I sliced off one of his fingers."

Mr. Eddie, not one to gloat after winning a bet, remained unchanged in demeanor, as he replied, "I figured a good slap and losing a fingernail would be enough. I thought his breaking point would be shallow. But let's face it, the sex part is what closed the deal. He might be in prison because he's a degenerate thief, but what he really is, is a cum freak. Let's get out of here and go grab a smoke."

Thirty-two

He dove down a rabbit hole gushing nonsense; a deep dive unveiling personal shortcomings derived from a platform of poor sourcing. It was his first time down this bleak hole. It would be his last. It wasn't worth it, with the thickest of thick skin required.

Johnny went online to research himself. Research was the wrong word. It was more like reading an uneducated diatribe of self, as he read opinion after untutored opinion regarding the subject matter keyed into the search engine: Johnny Blue.

The uncanny part, after reading several dozen scathing rants blasting his ineptness, was that the word that popped up all too frequently—more than he would've thought—was the word "radical," preceded as well as followed by a torrent of F-bombs, demeaning penis size comparisons, and creative anal violations.

For example: Johnny Blue is a small-dick radical fuck who needs his radical ass reamed with an oversized pinecone inserted sideways until it radically disappears. Take that, you radical brainless fuck. –Anonymous

In this not so clever example—a single snapshot that closely mirrored a majority of examples read—variations of the word radical won out 4-2 over forms of the word fuck; 4-1 over penis related comments; and 4-1 over sodomy references. Final count: a 4-4 split, with "radical" carrying an even load versus all other offensive words combined.

This forced him down another burrowed tunnel connected to our long-eared fury friend. But his new focus had nothing to do with self. Taking a completely different approach, he explored the R-word—and not the F-, P-, or A-word—which caused his online search to turn into an all-day session skirting the fringes of insanity while seriously seeking a nugget of knowledge.

Knowledge was what he sought, and, by day's end, knowledge was what he got. That elusive nugget was gifted by Angela Davis, the prominent counterculture and political activist, the academic, the author, whose run of counterculture notoriety dates back to the 1960s. Johnny found a quote online attributed to her, a short quote that summed it up: Radical simply means "grasping things at the root." A seven-letter, three-syllable word. A beautiful word with a simple meaning, a powerful meaning: "grasping things at the root."

But if ever conventional forces attached the word "radical" to your name, calling you a "radical" this or a "radical" that, then what they were really doing was labeling you as a subversive, an agitator, a loon, while conveniently withholding accurate descriptions such as critical thinker, problem solver, solution administrator, or bearer of truth to aid the masses. And they would never report whole truths because of their affinity for corporate dominance. Instead, swaying toward an ingrained nature of repeat and wait regardless of damage done—repeating misleading information while sitting back and waiting for the sheep to chime in with predictable responses.

Thirty-three

He remembered it clearly. Too clearly, as he replayed the mental reel. He was surprised by his own level of eye-opening shock. He truly was. "Son of a bitch. They got me, and I didn't see it coming."

As he walked out of the bathroom in a hotel room positioned high above San Francisco's Union Square, there stood two masked men, silently, patiently, waiting for him. How did I not know they were coming? Why had I not anticipated this obvious snare? Why had I not prepared for this exact situation?

FUUUUUCK! FUUUUUCK! FUUUUUCK!

And as they pointed their weapons at center mass, barreled weapons of death, he looked over at his two babies, rifle and handgun—at the ready and fully loaded—lying on one of two queen-size beds in the room he'd reserved for a three night stay; lying out of reach.

Feeling helpless was out of the ordinary for him. But he now felt that uneasiness wholeheartedly, as he knelt down naked in an unfavorable position. It sucked. Do as you're told. Maybe you'll live. Probably not.

The prick of a needle followed by a slow push sent him away. In a sense, he welcomed it. Deep down he had already surrendered. He was now part of someone else's plan.

In and out of consciousness, hands tied, hands untied. Face covered, always covered. One time, though, while sitting on the toilet and sipping water, he caught a glimpse. They had ditched their masks; lifting his so he could hydrate. One was a stranger, one was not. Where had our paths crossed? Flickering spots, shadows, then darkness. Almost.

Hazily awake. Hands untied while they maneuvered fingers. What were they doing? Oh, I know what they're doing. Shit, I am dead.

PART III

There's an old Irish saying that goes something like this:
"When you're about to be run out of town, get out in front and make it look like a parade."

Thirty-four

San Francisco. Union Square. The final campaign.

Leaflets in people's hands, on the ground and in trash cans. Purple in color with a simple message in black 16-point font: Cancel all social media accounts until those at the highest levels of responsibility implement fair and just policies. Where users of such platforms have a say-so in personal information shared, bartered. The lofty goal: A billion cancelations worldwide to get shareholder's monetary attention. One plus nine zeros. A hair shy of thirty percent total usership.

It was his longest speech ever. Not Fidel Castro long, but long for him. He gazed out into a packed city square; packed streets and alleyways extending as far as the eye could see. He was holding a purple pamphlet in his right hand as he steered toward conclusion.

Raising the pamphlet high in the air, he leaned into the mic and stated as a matter of fact, "There are eight billionaires on this planet who possess as much money as half the world's population—that population's total combined financial resources. Half of seven-point-something billion people and growing as I speak. Eight men, with six of those eight acquiring their wealth by way of information technology, information systems.

"If I mentioned their names you would probably know most of them. The remaining two billionaires either rely heavily on technology to efficiently run their business processes or have invested heavily in technology to grow their financial portfolios.

"I can't say this loud enough: They control an overabundance of information put forth to the world, some of which is personal information that their users—you and I—freely handover on social media platforms. And like our supposed political leaders, these so-called tech leaders, these new age executives, have undervalued the common people. So I ask you this, why would we support these billionaires by buying what they're selling?

"Also of concern, these same individuals repeatedly tell the same lie, claiming that the chessboard in their sphere of influence rests upon an equitable plane for all to compete on. That, my friends, could not be further from the truth because they own the two-toned board and its matching pieces outright. They also write the rules to the game. And those rules are everchanging so as to squash rising competition.

"Ask yourself how much it costs to rent or own a home right here in Silicon Valley's backyard? How many homeless people did you step over on the way to this event? Tell me this, why are the citizens of California—a state of forty million people whose economy ranks fifth worldwide—not being taken care of in terms of everyday basic needs? Forty million citizens paying the highest levied state income taxes in the country. Why do they not have affordable housing, equal education opportunities, living wages, broader local food supply access, more efficient transportation options, healthcare for all, and improved water and air quality? Why are their basic needs not being met?

"These tech leaders, whether they admit it or not, sway political thought by influencing political progress or the lack thereof—pressing for outcomes that benefit their interests and their interests alone. Research the top ten establishment media outlets and find out who owns and financially supports them. What do you think the 'MS' in MSNBC stands for? And who do you think owns the Washington Post? Those in charge of the mainstream narrative who withhold and subdue information, who discredit independent media sources, who manipulate algorithms at the expense of the people, are guilty of altering freethinking by restricting off-narrative information flow.

"So when these rich men and their like purposely mention their charitable work, their philanthropic ways—without being asked to do so, by the way—know this, they do it for the tax benefits and the false accolades and not to lessen or solve real problems. Charity attached to personal financial incentives and popularity is not charity. What it is, is a sales gimmick. It's false advertisement.

"If you garner awards because of your financial worth, then—to frame this in proper context—you've earned nothing. All you did was buy a fancy trophy. You purchased a hunk of shiny hardware after competing against no one. You're a fraud, as are your hangers-on.

"The solution to 'you-name-the-problem' already exists. What's lacking in solving major issues domestically and abroad is a power representation possessing courage, political will, and the execution of problem-solving measures. On top of that, leadership must actually care about the people in the form of action and results. To them, I say, 'Be done with your hollow words.'

"However, the masses, combining as one and focused on the betterment of society, have much more power than any political system, any corporation, or any military force. We—as in the people—simply need to organize nationwide with a common goal of siphoning corruptness from our political system. We must also exhibit a level of persistency that has never before been seen, felt, or heard. But more than that, we must be willing to die for worthwhile causes.

"The elite problem solvers of the past century—generally assumed to be leaders of the free world—failed to bring about real solutions to a host of menacing problems facing humankind; problems they created on the backs of bogus solutions. Rarely did they take into consideration the damage caused as the result of their greed. And if by slim chance adverse consequences were taken into account, they were quickly brushed aside so as to avoid stymieing monetary reward.

"They were never problem solvers to begin with; but rather, problem creators and excessive wealth hoarders. And when they died off, they left it to the next generation of elite pretenders to cause additional havoc while duplicating their predecessors in the form of greed, power, and lies.

"Frown at the word 'elite.' Be cautious and skeptical of elite society and the statues that celebrate their like. Our communities don't need the political elite—the corporate elite, the religious elite—telling us how to problem-solve. They are not our saviors and they never were. They are the antithesis of that word. They are our adversaries.

"It is up to common citizenry to solve those problems we did not create in the first place. What I call 'an inheritance of lies.' We simply need to organize and do the right thing for the people, for the planet, and ignore the entitled aristocrats who act out problem-solving measures around an accommodating tub of wealth while operating within a distorted system where power is conveniently tilted in their favor.

"Today's political and corporate leaders revolve around the same set of patent lies. They are sidewalk seers trying to convince the masses that the distorted future they profess is the only future. It's a scam. Ignore them, and welcome community."

The streets of San Francisco were alive. The roar for Johnny Blue and his powerful words was deafening, as he concluded his speech standing behind an unwanted podium. He took it all in, soaking up the reverberating energy in the square. Truth mattered. And so there he stood, stock-still, appearing content while remaining on stage a beat or two longer than usual.

When the shot rang out, echoing off a multitude of high-rise facades, there was no confusion as to what it was. With mass shootings on a decades-long rise, most Americans were familiar with what a gunshot sounded like. To be accurate: a single round fired from a rifle. The people in attendance certainly knew what it was. No confusion there. And with that, the crowded streets, sidewalks and alleyways bordering Union Square broke out into total chaos.

Panic is an interesting thing, as is survival. And when you combine the two in a tight setting then you can count on people getting trampled. With the exception of the receiver of the lone bullet, nobody died. But quite a few people were injured. Some bad, requiring hospitalization. And some not so bad and only requiring minimal attention.

Johnny Blue, the intended target, was dead. As in missing a section of head dead. It was not a sight to be seen, but certainly a scene that drew you in—JFK-like.

Thirty-Five

Shakes, with action cam positioned and focused, stayed with his assigned video coverage until the very end, and then at least a full minute after that, holding back tears until he was done recording the atrocity. He witnessed his friend's death at close distance. Too close a distance.

A video of the shooter, dead in a hotel room overlooking Union Square—murder and suicide weapons lying nearby—was mysteriously sent to an independent media source. It began bouncing across the Web within minutes after Johnny Blue's assassination. Hundreds of recordings captured by those in attendance were also racing wild across the Net; an assortment of angled video clips showing bullet impact and subsequent gnarly result.

The killer had been identified by an unknown journalist. The major news networks had been scooped by a recent university grad working from her basement apartment in upstate New York. She was thankful that she'd been easily convinced to back out of an earlier engagement, deciding instead to stay home with laptop and new puppy versus hanging out in a coffeeshop with friends nursing hangovers. Self-important media types were wondering how an unknown nobody got her grimy little hands on such a crucial piece of information before them.

The killer worked for a small agency within the U.S. government. His name was James Nolan. He was a former Marine sniper. He lived in Virginia and worked in D.C. She even listed the hotel name and room number from where he committed his heinous crime, to include exact details of the rifle and cartridge used.

News media vans and government agents were on their way to her apartment. Her new personal attorney—paid for by an anonymous source—was also heading her way and would be the first to arrive.

John Machado

And as the angry and ill-informed descended upon Syracuse, New York, Molly Cho, the independent journalist in question, furiously typed away at her keyboard while giving insight to the world a detailed bio on Mr. James Nolan. All the while Biscuit, her three-month-old puppy, slept soundly in her lap.

And the scramble was on. And a shitload of questions needed answering. And conspiracy theorists were chiming in with unresearched opinions. And major media talking heads were also chiming in with unresearched opinions. And government representatives were chiming in with weak-ass suppositions tied to antiviolence rhetoric, with oft repeated "thoughts and prayers" patter conveniently slid in to cover bases and check boxes. Basically, just another day in America.

Shakes and Moira made their way over to Lawyer Bill's office. Union Square was off limits, completely closed to the public. A major hotel was also cordoned off; yellow tape and barricades everywhere.

SFPD everywhere, with first responders mingling around a five-star hotel and doing as little as possible while waiting for the Feds to show up and flex muscle. Go ahead, it's all yours. The hierarchy within city hall wanted nothing to do with a brewing political shitstorm; reason being, it appeared as if a dead government employee and former Marine Corps sniper was the one who pulled off the successful sniping. Let the Feds sort it out.

It was now "Spin time," time for everybody and their brother to collectively spin the shit out of a story in its infancy. What a mess. But hey, this story would certainly sell tampons and stool softener and bathroom disinfectant for the next year and then some. Who doesn't revel in someone else's demise when in the business of doing just that? The vultures were circling, ready to pick, pick, pick at the carcass's cooling flesh.

Lawyer Bill refused all incoming calls; his phone ringing off the hook. There would be time for that later. Shakes and Moira handed over their smart devices to the old-time lawyer. The entirety of their electronic data was about to be thoroughly analyzed by a well-paid expert. Their respective tech gadgets and related content would never be handled or viewed by a single soul outside Lawyer Bill's purview.

Shakes and Moira would be leaving the city—why stay—but not until they were interviewed by the Feds in Lawyer Bill's presence. All communication requests connected to the Johnny Blue team would first go through Lawyer Bill and, who's kidding who, most likely end with the crafty lawyer as well. "Fuck 'em, feed 'em fish."#

Thirty-six

One down, three to go.

Getting out of the city was not difficult once they made the four block walk from hotel to parking garage. Like the rest of the herd they were ignored; two businessmen in navy blue suits wearing sunglasses and walking single file; outfitted in matching backpacks and moving at a predetermined pace. Their shoes, black cross trainers, could have been a giveaway if the right person took notice. But that didn't happen.

One headed north then east; destination, "The Silver State." The other, south then east—Fresno County bound. So far, so good.

He made it to the outskirts of Selma without a snag. He parked on a secluded dirt road, secured the vehicle and hiked into agriculture. He marched through grapevines, row after orderly row. Not grapes for winemaking, but grapes left to dry in the sun. Raisins.

Nobody saw him coming, at least not the intended target—a conservative congressman. Once he hogtied the congressman's wife and shooed away a yapping terrier the size of a wharf rat, he pointed the gun at the congressman's forehead. The boisterous, TV-tough-sounding politician was none of that as he waited, waiting to die and looking up at the masked man while avoiding direct eye contact. The trigger was pulled. Bullseye.

Back to the car. A cell phone removed from the trunk. Call made. Cell phone destroyed. Heading off to the Monterey Peninsula.

The liberal tech tycoon attempted to hide behind inflated ego, conducting himself as if speaking to top-level executive yes-people. But once punched in the mouth and manhandled to a kneeling position on the floor, he let go disrespectful tendencies due to lacking the needed skill set to defend himself against a practiced human being.

He, too, had to wait in fear for the trigger to be pulled. In the end he got what the congressman got: direct hit center forehead.

Three down, one to go.

Thirty-seven

There was rioting in the streets in a host of cities scattered across America, on the coasts and spread throughout the in-betweens. The U.S. government had some explaining to do. It looked as if they had a hand in the assassination of a radical activist: one Mr. Johnny Blue, now dead and entering full-on martyrdom as his legend grew by the second. T-shirts would soon be made.

On another bizarre note, a back-page story in a prominent West Coast newspaper revealed that a conservative congressman and a well-known billionaire tech executive had been assaulted in similar fashion. One while at home in California's central valley, the other at his coastal mansion on California's Monterey Peninsula.

Both had been shot with a paintball gun. Both in the forehead. Ouch. Both with blue paint. Blue? Interesting color choice. Then they were hogtied and left in uncomfortable ways; surprised they'd survived, embarrassed by predicament. And, oh, oh, oh, what a painful paint-splattered headache.

Oddly enough, it appeared as if the shooter then placed two phone calls from untraceable numbers as a heads-up to the authorities regarding each man's plight. Even odder, there were videos of both circulating the Web in what they thought to be their final minutes alive, as they cried and begged forgiveness for misrepresenting the people while openly admitting to dastardly deeds.

What in God's name was going on? Weird shit, right? And, what to do? Who knew?

So it began, full investigations into government agencies. Especially the agency that had employed James Nolan. Lawsuits were in the works, with Lawyer Bill plotting center in the mix of legal disarray. Government heads would soon roll.

Politicians were scrambling. Journalists were scrambling. Tech executives were scrambling. Protection for high-ranking politicians and important tech types was heightened—the overreaction of frightened rich people making it all about themselves—as they were unable to command personal insignificance.

The people, however, were more than angry. They were crazily pissed off, ignoring dusk to dawn government issued curfews staggered throughout major cities across the country—from Anchorage to Miami. The implementation of violent tactics was increasing as the people pushed back at elite society. Molotov cocktails seemed to be the attention getters of choice.

Fearing the worst, top ranking government officials publicly threatened Marshal Law. But it was not the time for issuing ultimatums. The people's retort: Bring it on but be prepared for total chaos and the shutdown of an entire nation.

And with that their bluff was called, as a series of Molotov cocktails were tossed inside occupied buildings (both government and corporate) by people wearing masks and referring to themselves as patriots; tossed at moving cars (cars belonging to multimillionaires and billionaires); tossed on private properties (DC politicians' front doors). We'll see your threat and raise you terror and susceptibility to injury and death. There was a slight leveling of the playing field.

In the end, cooler heads prevailed. Sensible government authorities finally listened to sound advice from a multitude of civic leaders and put the kibosh on spurious threats and plans. They abruptly shifted gears, leaning toward compromise by publicly expanding the net on needed investigations. And when in front of national audiences, they looked straight into the camera and promised full transparency along with truth and justice.

The people were skeptical. Of course they were. They'd heard those words before, in exact order and what amounted to a political broken record.

Hundreds of spokespeople from different areas of the country sprang up. New leaders. A fresh group of activists representing the people. Like Johnny Blue, they spoke about action, human rights and nonviolence. They also spoke to personal choice, not wanting to tell anyone how to conduct themselves in the quest for equality. Familiar words gaining momentum.

Two printed T-shirts became hot commodities. Different versions in blue and red. They were worn by the many seeking drastic change.

Blue shirt: WATCH OUT FOR GOVERNMENT SNIPERS
Red shirt: WATCH OUT FOR MOLOTOV COCKTAILS

Thirty-eight

I think of her often. Everyday. Love with her was beautiful. I want to be with her again. Maybe. On my way.

He headed back to where he wanted to be. He was calm. He was composed. He was relieved, and genuine in his thoughts while content with how things turned out.

Only seven people—five now—had partial semblance of what really happened. And four of the five still living had incomplete chapters in their personal diaries of understanding; reason being, they didn't know the whole story. The people, the elites, the government, had no clue as to what went down. And they never would.

Shakes Montoya, driving Johnny's motorhome, left the city; a companion in the passenger seat. Moira Montez also left the city, heading in the opposite direction.

Jake O'Malley stood behind the bar at O'Malley's. He felt contrasting emotions: accomplishment and loss. He downed a shot of thirty-year-old single malt Scotch whisky, then poured another.

Lawyer Bill stayed in the city. San Francisco was his home. Where he held court. Where he got shit done. From where he balanced control upon a hidden dais of true power.

Thirty-nine

I hid inside a church and peered through the opening of a stained glass window left ajar. I watched as he entered the parking lot, not yet knowing it was him. I watched because of roused intuition, as he slowly navigated the lot and parked about as far from the hall as you could possibly park while still remaining on church property. And even though he was wearing a hat and glasses, I recognized him straight away as he stood from the car and faced my direction.

He'd been groomed since childhood to be a damn good shot. And that he was. He was cocky, too.

In addition—during training, anyway—he showed a propensity to be uninterested in the details, the minutia. That was it. He wasn't lazy or complacent or lacking in other skill sets outside of hitting a target. He just happened to be the guy who was unmoved by what most other people had to say, because in his mind he already knew it all. And he didn't try to hide that simple fact; not with peers, not with instructors.

I was one of those instructors. And, between us, we regularly said the same thing about him, "He was a bit of an asshole, but man could he shoot." Our orders were to produce exactly that: highly skilled USMC Scout Snipers. He definitely fit the bill. But he had a flaw or two that might one day prove unfavorable.

It appeared as if he hadn't done his homework. Was he bluffing? I wasn't so sure. Deception or not, it was time for me to continue to do my homework. Time for me to turn it up a notch. Time for me to bring other people into the mix to assist with countersurveillance measures. I was still interested in all aspects of my job.

He did what I would have done, hovering at the edge of the first group of people preparing to leave—a cup and a napkin in one hand. Either he'd improved greatly, which meant he was fully aware of outside involvement (me in particular), or he'd decided against countersurveillance efforts altogether. He probably surmised Johnny Blue to be a schmo. I was glad Shakes was inside capturing video.

He didn't stick around once he got to his car, getting inside and leaving right away. Interesting. Time to make a few phone calls. I would be extra cautious until I knew for sure he'd returned from where he came.

What impressed me the most about Shakes was how he handled himself during that first encounter with James Nolan. Sure, he shot good video. And sure, Nolan didn't realize he was being videoed. But none of that was overly impressive.

The impressive part—the thing that can't be taught—was what drew Shakes to Nolan in the first place. And when I asked him that all-important question, he didn't hesitate in answering, saying, "I noticed him because there was nothing to notice, which was what separated him from the rest of the crowd."

My young, sharp-witted friend had arrived.

Forty

As he steered the motorhome down a gravel driveway, a driveway wide enough to fit a tractor-trailer, Shakes reflected on the initial spying of James Nolan. It was the beginning of the end, and, upon further reflection, he probably realized that well before Rob explained in detail the severity of the Nolan encounter. At the time, though, he felt a level of excitement that was also weighted in sorrow—a wanted challenge overshadowed by the underhanded ways of the world.

He remembered having a sudden awareness, an awareness as to the lengths powerful people would go to hinder the truth and squash freethinking. It was the adult version of finding out there is no Santa Claus. And apparently alternative solutions deemed radical have consequences attached to them. The repercussions surrounding deep-rooted, truthful speech originate with those doing the selective listening, the cunt-like prejudging, and the leveling of accusations just prior to dishing out penalties that don't fit the crime.

He also realized that to be a wether was to survive in the dark repeating the commonly repeated and acting as if you still had balls. But in the end, it's just an act. And Shakes couldn't live like that.

It's why he ran from poisoned relations reeking of sheep shit. Fuck that. Tell your truth and live in the light regardless of consequences. A limited number of people live that type of lifestyle; bravely existing on the margins of society.

And the bad, bad man getting coffee—acting as if he belonged in this sacred space for speaking, for listening—was a fraud, and a man who followed orders based on a stranger's rationale.

"Whose house is this?"

Shakes—returning to the now—looked over at his mother, and said, "This is my friend's sister's house."

"Is your friend meeting us here?"

"He drove with us. He's in a compartment in the back of the motorhome."

Katie turned toward Shakes, a look of bewilderment on her face.

Shakes added, "My friend is dead, mom. His ashes are in an urn. And you and I are delivering those ashes to his family."

"Was he a good man?" Katie asked.

Shakes reply, "He was the best of men."

Maria and Dr. Bob came out on the porch as the motorhome approached. She'd never met the young man but had read many a handwritten letter from her brother singing the praises of Shakes Montoya.

After parking, Shakes walked around to the passenger door, opened it, and helped his mom down from the raised seat. He then opened the side door and stepped back inside the motorhome.

As they walked toward the porch, Maria and Dr. Bob descended steps to greet them in the yard. Shakes placed the urn and a gym bag on soft soil before embracing husband then wife, holding Maria a beat or three longer than Dr. Bob, openly tearing up as he felt a familial presence. He introduced them to his mother—not entirely sure they were expecting her—before they turned toward the house to continue conversations, to officially pass off ashes and exchange gifts, to tidy up a bit, to enjoy a meal.

Forty-one

Moira Montez pulled up outside the Jiu-jitsu academy she'd trained at since early childhood, and what amounted to an on-again, off-again relationship since her Army days. After walking inside, she was touched by familiar smells: mats, human sweat, cleaning agents. A man in his sixties—lean, soft eyes, constrictor strong—walked up to her while greeting her in Portuguese, "Oi, tudo bem," and gave her a big hug. They hadn't seen each other in years.

She came to ask permission, get advice, bare a sad soul. They sat barefoot on grappling mats—a different office, a different world—undisturbed for hours. There were no classes scheduled that day, no private training sessions, just the murmur of voices and the creaks and groans of an aging building.

Her Jiu-jitsu master listened intently, giving sound advice when asked, offering permission when requested with logical conditions attached. Moira's only expectation was the want of nothing handed to her. And with this man, that was a given.

He advised that she sleep on it. Make no decisions today. Kick it around for a good while; at least a full week. There was no rush. He wanted her to make the best decision for her, for all involved, because if she said yes, then a lot of hard work and long hours were in her future. Moira said she'd get back to him in a week. She thanked him dearly, "Muito obrigado."

She already knew what her answer would be. But she had arrived at the academy with a deep-seated need to bounce thoughts and ideas off someone who possessed wisdom, internal strength, and paternal love for her. If given the opportunity at this stage in life, her answer was going to be, "Yes, I'm ready to make a total commitment and I'm ready to do the work." But she needed corroboration from that special person who could shine light on the correct roadmap for reaching destinations sought. And that is what she received.

Moira headed south. Time for another road trip. Time to get the feel of another geography. Time to heal.

Forty-two

He parked where he usually parked. After unlocking the container, he walked over to his most valuable possession. It rested where he'd left it—on a metal shelf. He placed it on top of an industrial workbench, removed a pen and notepad from a steel drawer, sat down, and began writing.

His written instructions were concise. Oyster Joe would appreciate that. When done, he mused, 'That was much easier than I thought it was going to be; really not that complicated when lawyers aren't involved.'

He reorganized an already organized container, wanting the order of things to seem obvious, to seem logical for first time viewers and eventual disseminators of stuff—his stuff. He went from container to trailer and removed everything that sniffed of personal possession, to include clothes and used linen. That took less than ten minutes.

He bagged garbage and a host of other items he deemed nonessential, filling two trash bags with an assortment of odds and ends. After tying off each bag with a tight square knot, he stacked them in a wheelbarrow and rolled the single-wheel cart over to the far side of the barn; stashing it there.

Lastly, he dealt with his car, removing items such as sunglasses, air freshener sticks, loose change, and anything other than required documents. He sat on the car's hood and took a personal inventory—mental, physical. He was ready to move on to the next thing.

Naked, he retrieved a few useful tools and a burlap sack containing two items. He fired up the tractor and drove to his special spot. The drive from trailer to grave took around eight minutes on the small tractor, a slow drive and not a drive that unfolded in a straight line. It took about the same amount of time to get there on foot.

Once there, he nudged the bulky lid farther than usual. He killed the engine, stepped from the small tractor and walked over to inspect the marker. It was in fine shape.

He lowered himself inside the grave, the burlap sack tied loosely around secondary wrist. He untied the sack and placed it on cold earth at head of grave. Standing tall, he extended both hands above his head and firmly pressed callused palms up into rusted steel. He set his feet and readied his legs.

Almost there. He visualized precise motion and, when the time was right, performed three powerful lower body thrusts while shuffling his feet in the same direction. He moved the hunk of metal back into place, covering the entire opening.

It was dark inside but for wily threads of natural light. He sat down next to the sack, removed a small box and began speaking—a conversation with her.

Forty-three

Politics played at the highest levels of government can be easily compared to children throwing temper tantrums while immersed in playground disputes.

The current president had no knowledge as to what transpired within the little-known agency that employed James Nolan prior to his termination (literally). The agency had been designed to do just that, put distance between top brass and secret goings-on. In addition, the president's opposition screamed of same political affiliation between Nolan, the agency director, and the president himself. Noise aside, they were only stating the obvious.

Newly educated by staff members, the president let it be known that this obscure agency was formed under the opposing party's power not so long ago. It was their fault. Not his.

Acting as if insulted by the president's political gamesmanship—and with little counterargument to speak of—opposition mouthpieces repeated their high-volume whine of like party alliance and an abhorrent event transpiring on the president's watch regardless of who, what, where, when, and why the named agency was formed in the first place.

When cornered by the media, the director of the agency in question, a director appointed by the current president, stated that he did not know a James Nolan and that this man was obviously a rogue agent. He went on to say that he had zero recall regarding any dubious missions assigned under his leadership: "I know nothing." Problem was, his position on the power ladder didn't extend quite high enough. Rarely are you thrown a lifeline when ignorance is your best defense, especially when the politically elevated are actively covering their collective asses.

It was an easy decision for the professionally exposed. The director of the little-known agency, an agency that mainstream media outlets had rarely, if ever, reported on, was let go—as in fired, with his political career abruptly snuffed out, to include the strong possibility of a future arrest for a series of unthinkable crimes. The ex-director was the scapegoat that would suffer society's wrath. Let the courts and the lawyers and public opinion sort it out. Shit definitely rolls downhill.

That was not enough for the people, though, as a million strong protested in the form of a march on the nation's capital one Saturday morn. And with terrible optics reflecting off the people's pushback—and with the world looking on—the entire small agency that once supported James Nolan was completely shut down, eliminated, with no real political backlash from either side of the aisle. A win-win for those politically concerned.

The people were painlessly quieted by behind the scenes jockeying that cost the decision makers nothing, no collateral damage whatsoever. However, from the few possessing the ability and will to exercise critical thinking, it begged the question: Why was this agency formed in the first place? Arriving at a straightforward answer bellowed difficult, because there wasn't a simple answer to this fundamental question. The hard truth was intertwined with a bevy of complicated and disturbing answers. It would take an independent journalist with craft fortitude and time—a whole bunch of time—to begin fitting the pieces together in an intricate jigsaw puzzle that the mighty didn't want solved.

Intricate, because James Nolan worked for an agency within an agency. And just because the subset agency was eliminated did not mean that its mother agency wouldn't continue on as if nothing had happened. In fact—due to very strong forces—its continuance was certain, if not guaranteed.

For the most part, that's all it takes to commit crimes at the highest levels of government. Simply employ a game of Three-card Monte and count on a citizenry low expectation that doing very little will be enough as long as it can be spun as going above and beyond. And that in a nutshell is the history of American politics at its worst.

Forty-four

Shakes took the long way, the beautiful way, driving up the Oregon coast from Brookings to Seaside and beyond, with a scattering of coastal cities in between. They stopped at campgrounds along the way for overnight stays, son and mother enjoying their first ever vacation of sorts but refusing to label it as such. It just was.

Katie was much different in new surroundings away from crowded populations. She appeared to be calmer. And Shakes was at ease because she was at ease. They were enjoying themselves.

Their final coastal trek had them crossing a bridge at the mouth of the Columbia river that connects Oregon to Washington; connecting Astoria to Point Ellice. They traversed a four mile span above nature's mightiness, where powerful river meets dominant ocean.

At last they headed east, heading inland toward a woodsy township in Washington. They eventually hugged the far edges of southwestern Puget Sound, not far from Oyster Joe's place.

Moira took a walk down the pier. Unhurried, she stopped at different spots along the uneven planks to observe the ocean, the beach, the birds. A thick marine layer hid the sun, making the ocean appear gray and cold because it was. There was something about this beach town that begged her return. She didn't know why, exactly, but that didn't matter because a magnet does what a magnet does.

She walked from pier to town, not a great distance, and stopped in front of an empty storefront. She perused a sign hanging in the window, eventually taking a pic with her phone. After making a quick phone call, she headed up to the main drag—the Pacific Coast Highway.

She continued another minute or so and finally stopped at a local coffeehouse with a catchy name: Coastal Mud. With coffee in hand, Moira went outside to enjoy the ocean smells and the strong brew. The crisp air offered renewed vitality as she sat down on a weather-beaten bench—her hair made messy by the breeze. Somewhat startled, she looked at her vibrating phone before tapping the screen and answering the incoming call.

Her instincts proved correct. Not wanting to dwell too long on good fortune, she decided to make another call. He didn't pick up. Not a big deal.

She just wanted to talk to somebody. So she made a second call, dialing the Reno number. He usually answered her calls, and, when he didn't, always called back within minutes.

Forty-five

The offsite meeting took place in a cabin tucked away in the Blue Ridge Mountains of Virginia. Four men attended the meeting, a meeting they deemed "private" while avoiding the word "secret." Semantics. A meeting that those at the highest levels of government would not know about. Nobody outside the cabin would know about it.

The meeting revolved around what really happened to James Nolan. He was ordered to assassinate Johnny Blue. They knew this because they gave the order in an indirect way that wouldn't lead back to the source. And—bottom line—they got what they wanted.

More importantly, they were privy to the autopsy report concerning Mr. Nolan as well as his detailed notes up to three days before he died. And the two major takeaways that came from those medical findings were the trace amounts of strong narcotics found in Nolan's expired body and the slight yet visible bruises on his wrists and ankles.

Moreover, the investigation revealed that Nolan's fingerprints were the only fingerprints found in the hotel room where the triggers were pulled. Not one other set of prints was discovered in the entire room. Not one. Rarely, if ever, is housekeeping that good. That in itself would have been an impossibility under normal circumstances.

None of that information was made public nor shared with bought and paid for media outlets. That would never happen. The flock had calmed down—happy to have pushed for justice and handed a political beheading, happy to have been the catalyst behind the closure of a government agency. They thought they got what they wanted. Fools so easily fooled.

"Then who fuck'n killed Johnny Blue if not our guy?" All four agreed that it was someone from their own government. Had to be. Someone who knew what Nolan was up to.

Holy shit! Who? Don't know.

They were 99.9% sure their involvement could not be uncovered. But that damn point-one percent was causing sleepless nights.

Blue's bodyguard and personal assistant were in the audience when the shot rang out. But more than that, they were low-level cronies at best. The lawyer? Definitely a greasy dude, but that was not the type of thing he'd get involved in. Check, check, and check.

Then who? We are definitely missing something here. And, whoever did it was a highly competent long-range shooter. Military or former military for sure.

Let's look into it further. We'll use one of our own. Someone dispensable. We won't give him all the facts, but we won't keep him in the dark, either. Maybe he'll uncover that one piece of information that clues us in to who we're really dealing with. It's worth a shot, but on the QT, and we will pull the plug ASAP if it gets complicated or if someone asks one too many questions.

Three of the four were in agreement. The lone holdout advised that they let it go. Move on as if nothing happened. The others said they would do just that, but not until a few questions were answered.

The majority decision won out.

Forty-Six

The pain I felt when you died was a pain attached to lost love. The pain I felt when I first met you was a pain of wanting love—a first-time feeling.

I'd read about love, heard songs relating to love, and observed Hollywood's version of love. But that initial feeling into uncharted waters when I first met you made me want it; no, crave it that much more. Yet, at that very same moment, I seriously considered taking the path of out-and-out avoidance. In all honesty, I was scared of the unknown.

To me it was like the allure of an accomplished painting or words on a page that affect you deeply, where the overwhelming emotion can't be explained. And once you've had that experience, you're glad you did knowing full well precise replication is impossible.

There was pain involved in being with you, too. That pain was tied to fear. The fear of losing you. My own insecurities pushing to the forefront. Something I never discussed with you. Funny how that works.

And then when I found out I was going to lose you, well, let me say this, I denied that possibility altogether. There was no way a just world would take you. Not you. Me? Of course. Go ahead. I've done some atrocious things. But not my only love. Not my angel. No way.

That's where I was wrong. There is no "fair" when it comes to death. No "fair" at all. If you're lucky, really lucky, there are brief moments of joy followed by the harsh realities of the world. I'm so glad I got lucky and found you. I love you, baby.

With their conversation complete, Rob Zamora opened the urn and poured her ashes onto wet earth. He spread them around, kneading her remains into mud and skin. Once done, he removed the final item from the burlap sack. An item he was all too familiar with.

He placed the sack over his head and rolled to one side, lying in the fetal position. He gripped the gun and moved it underneath the bristly canvas until the barrel pressed into the rehearsed spot. Holding tight the sack with his free hand, he closed his eyes and pulled the trigger.

Forty-seven

Shakes parked in the driveway, avoiding the wooded way in due to size of vehicle. It would be an easy steer from driveway to trailer's side once the old-timer opened the gate. But first, introductions: Katie, Oyster Joe.

After getting settled, Shakes and Joe took a walk in the woods while Katie familiarized herself with the Airstream trailer and the wide open space. Her new home. Free to stay if she wanted to stay. No obligations. No rules. Just live.

As they navigated around heavy thicket, Shakes spied the marker hanging in a tree. It triggered reflection, feeling the pain of loss before witnessing proof of loss. Getting closer, the scene began to open up—a sub-compact Kubota tractor, a sizable mound of dirt, a rusted metal slab resting on the ground. They stopped several yards from their friend's grave.

Joe: Everything you need is right here. There're extra tools in the bucket. I'm going to sit this one out. I'll choose to remember him the way I knew him to be, the way I saw him last. I loved that man.

Shakes: I understand. I'll do it first thing tomorrow morning.

Joe: Give the marker to your lady friend.

Shakes: I'll do that.

Joe: And when you're done, park the tractor outside the barn door. I'll handle it from there. It's going to take you a while to drag that hunk of steel out of the woods. Remember, there's no hurry. Take it slow, just like we taught you. And could you do me a favor?

Shakes: Of course.

Joe: Mark one of these trees close by. Discreetly, but permanently. Up high, maybe twenty feet. I'll be checking on him from time to time. Especially when I need to talk to somebody.

Shakes: Consider it done.

The meeting of five.

The only time they were ever together—anywhere. The grand plan was unveiled for the second time. They sat around a mammoth table, a beautifully lacquered conference table that Lawyer Bill comically compared to the size and shape of North Dakota. The longtime lawyer sat at head of table, two on each side: Johnny Blue and Shakes Montoya to his right, Moira Montez and Rob Zamora to his left.

Bill began the meeting, straddling a line of brevity before passing it off to Johnny Blue. It was his show. And just as he'd shared with Rob way back when—sitting on a rental car's hood and staring at his friend's back—he now shared with the other three.

When he was done there was complete silence in the room, as the newly informed processed what they'd just been told. This was not a joke. This was total commitment, and the first and final meeting open to any type of discussion.

Lawyer Bill ended the awkward silence: "Any questions?"

"Do you have any questions?" Moira fired back sarcastically, easing the tension as everyone laughed.

"I do not," replied the counselor, placing a cigar in his mouth and reaching for his lighter.

Johnny jumped in with, "Then let's move on."

And they did move on, as the smallest of details were unfolded. Their roles were explained. A complete game plan was set forth. At the end, Johnny thanked them for being part of his team, thanked them for fully vowing to the cause. He wrapped it up with these words:

"We don't want to be the tellers of someone else's story. We are not observers sitting in the stands. None of us would ever want that because we are the players in the game. A serious game. So remember, we are the creative doers responsible for an alternative solution based on action, an action most people yearn for but, in reality, fear.

"With that said, be proud of the fact that we've created our own story, a story that only a legitimate and committed investigative journalist could possibly piece together and make whole. And they would need a huge dose of luck as well as a proper nudge in the right direction to even get close to uncovering partial truths.

"Which means, no outsiders will know what really happened. Ever. Very few, a connected few still living, will know most of the story—the minute details that we are about to execute.

"My dear friends, I'm perfectly fine with that. We should all be fine with that. Let it become folklore."

That was the last they spoke of it; the last time they were all together. From that day forward they had a new focus and a new direction. And they would carry out their designed plan step by step just like it was diagrammed.

And tomorrow came. Too soon. But time to get on with it despite the degree of difficulty. Emotional difficulty.

As he walked away from the motorhome he saw a light on in the trailer. He was hoping that she liked it here, hoping she could be happy here. He took his time walking through the woods, wondering what Rob was thinking in his final minutes. Fear? Relief? What?

Shakes didn't waste any time upon arrival. After properly positioning the tractor and fastening the chains, he reversed slowly in a straight line until the opening was fully exposed. His heart began racing as he stepped from the tractor and walked that way, settling at foot of grave just like they'd discussed.

He looked because he needed to look. That's just the way it is sometimes. He took in the entire scene until permanently stamped into memory—glad that his friend's head was covered with a sack.

He disconnected the chains at the tractor and looked around. It was a tight clearing, but just enough room to maneuver in. Shaking his head from side to side, he thought, 'Rob was one smart motherfucker.' Then he began laughing, crying—bent over with hands on knees.

Once composed, he began the repetitive task of back and forth, filling the grave with earth from where it came. Funny thing was, he began at foot of grave, not wanting to rush the process before volume of dirt won out—a visual connection as the hourglass wound down.

And once he could see only dirt and not a speck of human skin, he felt a profound sense of relief, of understanding.

At completion, there was more dirt than space to fill. Not unusual nor a problem. For the time being there would be a swell of raw earth. That and the permanent marker would make it easier for Oyster Joe to find. In a year or so the mounded dirt would settle and become overgrown with vegetation.

By the time he stopped at the barn it was dusk. Where had the time gone? He looked toward the trailer and saw his mom standing outside its only door.

She waved. He waved back. She seemed happy.

Forty-eight

She drove up, taking two days to get there—fifteen and a half hours of drivetime to cover a thousand miles, give or take. One overnight stay and plenty of contemplative windshield time. She would drive straight through on the return trip, only stopping for gas and to use the restroom when absolutely necessary.

Shakes had called and said he needed to give her something. He added that it was a surprise and not a ploy and that catching a flight was out of the question.

Moira laughed at him for using the word ploy; told him as much between chuckles. She'd rather drive than fly anyway. It had been at least nine months since the last time they'd been together.

She ended it with, "I need to run something by you and doing it in person will be much better. This way works out well. See you in three days."

After meeting Katie, after sipping from a fresh cup of coffee, she followed Shakes from trailer to motorhome so they could take care of business.

Moira: So, what do you have for me?

Shakes: That (as he pointed at two brown packages stacked on a nearby countertop).

Moira: What is it?

Shakes: A gift from Johnny Blue.

Moira: And?

Shakes: The small one contains a million bucks. The bigger one, two million. You're looking at three million in cash. The big one is yours.

Moira: Are you fucking with me? Please tell me you're lying.

Shakes: I'm not lying. I got the same package, as did Johnny's sister and his two nieces. Oyster Joe got a package for a million, and you need to give the smaller package to your friend in Reno; also a cool million. Lawyer Bill set me up with an urn and seven packages from Johnny Blue. I left San Francisco with Johnny's ashes and twelve million dollars in cash stashed in a secret compartment in this very same motorhome.

Moira: No shit?

Shakes: No shit. And I have something for you from Rob, too.

Moira: Please tell me it's not money.

Shakes: It's not money (she didn't look convinced). Really, it's not money. It's actually a couple of things and I'll give them to you later.

Moira: You buried him?

Shakes. Yeah.

Moira: By yourself?

Shakes: Yeah.

Moira: Was it tough?

Shakes: Very.

Moira: I'll bet. I don't think I could have done it.

Shakes: He prepared me for it, plus it needed to get done.

Moira: Did you look?

Shakes: Yeah. I had to.

Mora: Also tough, I'm sure.

Shakes: Not as tough as losing a friend. And I didn't even know him that long.

Moira: Didn't matter how long you knew him. If you were his friend, if he let you in, then you were his friend for life. It's the way he was, loyal and quite the fuck'n character.

Shakes: That he was. Let's get out of here and head his way.

After arriving, she asked Shakes to show her exactly where he was buried. Looking at what was still evident to him—an outline of sorts—Shakes eyed the barely noticeable rectangular hump now covered in young vegetation. He walked to the head of grave and adjusted his position until directly above where he figured Rob to be, where he'd remembered seeing him last. Then he said, "Right here."

Moira walked over to where Shakes stood, gently nudged him out of the way, and took a seat on the cushioned flora mere feet above where her old grappling partner rested. She looked up at Shakes, and said, "Give me about ten minutes to be alone with him." Without commenting, Shakes removed Rob's dog tags from around his neck and handed them to Moira. And as he walked deeper into the woods, she began to weep, to sob.

They sat in lawn chairs just outside the shipping container's two large doors, enjoying more coffee and the crisp, fresh air. Shakes had propped the painting up against a stool so they could admire it in natural light.

Moira: He wanted me to have this painting in particular?

Shakes: Yeah. He left Oyster Joe detailed instructions of who got what.

Moira: It's beautiful.

Shakes: It is. I couldn't quite make it out at first glance, not completely. But after staring at it for a while, the whole thing came into view—a woman lying in bed looking out the window. There's something about this painting that makes you want to keep on staring at it; the different shades of blue, the varying degrees of light.

Moira: There's a subtle sexiness to it. And a certain innocence, too. It's beautiful. I know exactly where to hang it.

Shakes: Before you forget, what was it that you wanted to run by me?

Moira: Oh, that's right, I came here to ask you something that has nothing to do with a shitload of money. I hope I don't disappoint you.

Shakes: You're not the disappointing type.

Moira: Not yet, anyway. Listen up. I have a proposal for you. And it's going to take time, commitment, and a temporary relocation on your part.

Shakes: Let's hear it.

Moira: Okay, here goes. I started my own Jiu-jitsu academy down in Pismo Beach. I'm affiliated with my original instructor and I drive up to Monterey and train with him once a week because I'm getting ready to test for my black belt.

Shakes: Congratulations.

Moira: Shut up and listen. I'm competing again, teaching fulltime and living in a studio apartment directly above my academy. And I'm really digging it.

Let me lay it out for you. I want you to come down and train with me for three months and then test for your blue belt. We've gone this far together and it's important for me to promote you to the next level. I also know that it's a selfish request and that your mom is living up here with you and that you have other commitments. I'm not so sure you should leave her even for a short period of time. I want to do the right thing and I want you to do what's right for you and your mom. What do you think?

Shakes: I'd love to do that. I need a break from here and I also need to figure out where I'm going to eventually land. My mom is fine up here. She has her own place. Oyster Joe is fine with her living here, fine with having a neighbor. Everybody is in agreement that she can stay if she wants to stay. And so far, she's feeling this place—if you know what I mean. No crowds, nature, a kind of serenity. I'm the one who needs to figure shit out.

Moira: Cool. Sounds like it's a go. When do you want to come down?

Shakes: I could be down there a week from Monday. You good with that?

Moira: Perfect. Let's do it. You can park the motorhome in a private lot directly behind my place. I know the guy who owns the lot and he'll be cool with you parking it there for a few months. I'll give you a key so you can use the bathroom and the shower at the academy whenever you need to. It'll be a short walk from the motorhome to the back door. And remember, I'll be your instructor so no fucking.

Shakes: Right this second, you're not my instructor.

Moira: True. Do you have any condoms?

Shakes: Yeah, a whole box.

Moira: Grab two and let's take a walk in the woods.

As she was set to leave the following morning, Moira was a little nervous about driving a thousand miles with three million bucks stashed in the trunk of her car. Shakes told her to forget about the money, that it was just a couple of packages in the trunk of a car. Nothing else. A lot of people are driving around with shit in their trunks (no pun intended). Then he told her what to do with the money once she got to Pismo.

She asked, "Isn't that illegal?"

Shakes reply, "Only if you get caught. And then you'll have to pay a shitload of taxes before going to prison. But what else are you going to do, hide it under your mattress? So do it, and don't get caught."

She would open a safety deposit box upon her return to Pismo Beach.

Forty-nine

He hadn't seen hide nor hair of Mr. Eddie in weeks. He tried to make contact but was strongly warned against it. Now what?

Nathan Blue was released from prison on a dreary Wednesday morning. And after taking that first step into freedom, he was overcome with fear. Routine was no longer routine.

He took a bus to the nearest town and checked in at a cheap motel. The room was paid for by his sister. Suddenly he wanted to cry, and, oddly enough, he missed his prison cell.

The first thing he did was undress and take a long hot shower, scrubbing the smells of institution off every inch of skin. Once done, he got dressed and took a walk down Main Street.

He stopped in at a diner and ordered a heap of food: eggs, bacon, sausage, hash browns, biscuits & gravy and pancakes. He ate it all, coating everything in butter and syrup and gravy. No problem wolfing it all down, unable to fill hunger's void.

After checking to see what time it was, he paid up and made his way back to room number 112. She'd be awake by now. He called from the phone in the room. Collect. She answered on the second ring and accepted all charges.

They exchanged awkward pleasantries like adult siblings do when a relationship is beyond repair. She sat anxiously at a computer—left foot tap-tap-tapping hardwood floor—ready to do what he needed her to do.

He patiently gave detailed instructions while she methodically pressed black keys with hesitant fingers. Computers were not her strong suit, but being a grower and a nurse and a mom were. She eventually got to where he needed her to get to.

He asked for the exact figure. She told him what it was. He asked her to repeat it even though he heard her just fine the first time.

She repeated the number. He wrote it down using a cheap motel pen and notepad. He stared at it. They said their goodbyes.

He undressed and took another shower. This time he wasn't thinking about cleanliness. With soap he lathered his firm erection, masturbating for the first time in many months where he was free to fantasize without worrying about someone walking in on him. He came hard thinking dirty thoughts.

He dried off sitting naked on the bed. He thought about napping but decided against it. Instead, he picked up the notepad and read it out loud: "One dollar."

Then he thought, 'One dollar, equal to four quarters, or ten dimes, or twenty nickels, or one hundred pennies. Sixty-three million dollars gone.'

A phone cord, the bathroom door, and gravity took care of the rest. Nathan Blue died homeless and alone, broke but for a dollar to his name.

Fifty

She made the call after crossing over into California, her third state in seven hours. He picked up right away.

Moira: I have something for you.

Jake: And what might that be, young lady?

Moira: I hear a trace of nastiness in your tone.

Jake: Is that what you hear?

Moira: It is, but I have something for you that's much better than pussy.

Jake: Well, I only know two things better than pussy.

Moira: And what might they be? Please, educate me.

Jake: Thirty-year-old single malt Scotch whisky and money.

Moira: Well, then, I'm guessing I have one of those two things and it has nothing to do with spirits from the land of Scots, my friend. I'm heading back to Pismo from Shelton right now. I just entered California. When can you make it over to the coast so I can give you what's yours?

Jake: Tomorrow afternoon, say, around two.

Moira: I'll see you then. But one last thing, I'm going to need some financial advice.

Jake: Not a problem. We'll have plenty of time to take care of all your needs. See you tomorrow.

Moira: Bye.

Fifty-one

Shakes Montoya sat in a motorhome and watched as his mom played with two dangerous dogs. They made her part of their pack the very first time they detected her scent and sized her up. A connection. A bond.

Sitting back, he reflected on that first trip up north. Good times. Himself. Rob. Oyster Joe. He was there to learn, but they couldn't get enough instruction from him regarding his video setup. Funny how that worked out.

Oyster Joe was a good man like Rob Zamora was a good man. Shakes thought about how lucky he was to have met them. And that would've never happened if not for a chance encounter in a coffeeshop in San Francisco.

He would go down to Pismo Beach and train for three months. He would do that for her. But then he'd leave and find his own way. For some reason Canada was on his mind, specifically British Columbia.

Listen to your intuition. Head north. At least check it out. What do you have to lose?

Both dogs shot to attention as soon as he stepped from the motorhome, each staring him down in their own canine way. He laughed and they came running directly at him. He, too, was part of the pack.

He walked over to Oyster Joe's house, knocked on the side door and walked in when invited to do so. They talked for a bit, Shakes running future plans by the wise old man. Joe listened, offered up sound advice, and told the younger man that he'd figure it out on his own soon enough.

His mom was safe there. Safe as she'd ever be. Safe with distance from harmful family ties.

Fifty-two

He was high-tech savvy and young, especially when compared to the "old fuckers" he worked with, most of whom were in their forties, fifties and early sixties—a group of seasoned veterans who would take serious umbrage with his uninventive take on middle age. They chose him because of his propensity to outshine the competition and because he was expendable. When young looks down on old, formidable, ill-tempered old seeks payback.

He went by a few names, but the name most people settled on, besides Dickhead, was Smitty. To start things off, Smitty gained access to the Mother of all federal databases. He followed that up by gathering the names of all government snipers dating back fifty years—dead or alive. Next, he did a quick sort and separated living from dead, active from retired. And after a brief perusal, he shit-canned the dead guys and focused on those still breathing.

Closing in, he put to bed the active sniper file and concentrated on retired snipers only. He had a hunch. He plugged in those retired snipers who were originally from the state of Nebraska and eliminated the ones over sixty-five. He hit on seventeen guys. In the end he simply searched cities in Nebraska from where the retired snipers hailed. And, lo and behold, only one guy was from the same hometown matching Johnny Blue's.

Bingo. Robert Anthony Zamora. Pretty much the same age as Johnny Blue, too. What were the overwhelming odds that these two gents were familiar with each other? The answer to that question fell somewhere in the neighborhood of 99.99% affirmative.

Smitty made a few inquiries and one request, and within three days received a confidential file on Mr. Zamora. After hours upon hours of reading every bit of boring information stuffed inside a military personnel file, he hit pay dirt. It was right there in black and white: Zamora was once an instructor at a sniper school during the identical time that James Nolan was a student at that very same school.

Damn straight! File the report and go find Zamora.

Smitty was standing in Moyie Springs on a hot summer day. He could not believe how long it took to get from the East Coast to this northeastern Idaho shit-town; the better part of a day, to include three flights and a lengthy drive out into the middle of nowhere.

He was not a seasoned field agent. That said, he was not used to the pains associated with travel while journeying to remote country and sleeping in a shitty motel. To him it was as if Podunk America was something you read about in an overblown, feel-good novel. 'Fuck me,' he thought, 'this working in the field bullshit is overrated.'

Smitty followed the United States Postal Service path to Rob Zamora's mail landing, a rural post office located where Idaho and Montana bump shoulders. He walked in the very second they opened for business and immediately inquired about a specific postal box while launching into a poorly rehearsed, made-up story about trying to find his uncle. The lone government employee responsible for working the early shift patiently listened to Smitty's entire pathetic story. And when Smitty finally shut up, the clerk, without hesitating or considering confidentiality in the least—because small towns are nothing like big cities—openly shared that the box in question belonged to Jerry Rasmussen. Then he told him where Jerry lived.

With a boost of confidence spilling over into arrogance, Smitty came to the inexperienced conclusion that this field agent crap wasn't as tough as those old fuckers told him it was going to be. All you had to do was skillfully lie and ask the right questions. Re-energized, he headed over to Jerry Rasmussen's place.

In the company of big trees, he exited a two-lane road and turned left onto a cobblestone driveway, a driveway that was a good fifty yards long with a right-leaning bend leading up to an open three-car garage. Jerry Rasmussen was standing in the garage waiting. Apparently small-town Americans have cellphones.

Smitty got out of the car and made eye contact with the lone gentleman looking back at him. He opened with, "Howdy," having never before used that greeting in his entire life. Rasmussen, seeming friendly enough, said, "How're you doing," and then said that Big John, the postal clerk, called and told him that yours truly was on his way over to the house.

Smitty gave him the "looking for my uncle" story and Rasmussen acted as if he was interested in every word despite having already received the complete lowdown from Big John. They chatted for a while and Rasmussen explained to Smitty that Zamora's mail was definitely forwarded to his P.O. box. Problem was, he didn't know a Rob Zamora. He'd attempted to put a stop on "this other guy's mail," but that turned into a whole complicated mess with the USPS. So, in the end, he said, "Fuck it," and simply trashed Zamora's mail whenever he received it. And that happened less and less as time went on.

In Smitty's mind, Jerry Rasmussen appeared to be telling the truth. He would run a thorough background check on the guy later, but he certainly seemed to be on the up and up. Smitty had traveled to this ass-backwards town to find out that Zamora had completely dropped off the radar while simultaneously throwing a monkey wrench into the works by covering his tracks in case someone came looking. Zamora was definitely up to no good. Bingo for the second time.

Smitty thanked Jerry for his time and made his way back to that shitty motel. This cross-country travel stuff was kicking his ass. After a solid night's sleep, he'd drive back to the tiny airport that got him within reasonable driving distance of Moyie Springs and catch a flight to Seattle. He was going to pay a visit to the only home Rob Zamora ever owned, as well as the town he'd lived in since retiring from the Marine Corps: Shelton, Washington.

Jerry Rasmussen followed instructions well, which was one of the many traits that made him good at his job: a finish carpenter. He waited an hour before driving down to the only grocery store in town; a pocket full of quarters in tow. He sat and waited a good half hour, paying attention to the comings and goings of those who came and went. Nothing appeared out of the ordinary.

Jerry used a payphone to make the call. He told the man on the other end that a stranger showed up at his place pretending to be the nephew of a man he did not know but for junk mail. And, believe it or not, the out-of-towner never offered up his name. Jerry spoke to his unwanted visitor's height, weight, overall appearance, and the key discussion points covered while they talked in his garage. The other man said, "You did good. I'll send you a little something-something in a few days." Jerry thanked him and hung up.

Oyster Joe received a call from an unfamiliar voice. Rob had prepared him for this exact situation. He listened to every word, using a No. 2 pencil to jot down notes in the front page margin of a six-day-old newspaper. And as their conversation concluded, he thanked the man and told him he'd receive a package in the mail soon enough. The man thanked Oyster Joe and hung up.

Shelton was much bigger than Moyie Springs. It was more of a depressed small city than a depressed small town. And Smitty preferred bigger over smaller because it made it easier to blend in. He grabbed a bite to eat on the fly and drove up to Rob's former residence while eating a fast-food burger and washing it down with a diet cola.

Once there, he got out of the rental car and took in an expanded view of Puget Sound. Very nice. A man and a woman came out of the house and Smitty apologized for the surprise visit while introducing himself as Rob Zamora's nephew. They introduced themselves as Dan and Dierdre. Neither one had ever had the pleasure of meeting Rob.

Dan said, "The real estate agent who sold us the house didn't really mention him. The bottom line, this place was in the right location at the right price and in good condition. I mean, check out the view." Smitty acknowledged the beautiful view.

Dan then said, "There was a rumor floating around town that he was staying at an old oyster farmer's place for a short time. But who knows if that was true or just gossip?"

Smitty asked, "Do you know the farmer's name?"

Dan said, "That's easy: Oyster Joe. He lives a few miles from here."

Dierdre spoke up, "But I hear he's not the type of man you just drop in on. He's well-guarded and private."

"Well-guarded?" replied Smitty, with a questioning look on his face.

Dan, hankering to be the man in the know, felt the need to clarify what his wife had just said. She hated that about him. "I think what my wife is trying to say is that he has two big dogs and he lives on a private road that leads to a dead end. He has no neighbors. So, for most folks, there's no reason to go down that road unless invited."

"If it's not an inconvenience, could you give me directions to his place?" Smitty asked.

Dan looked at Dierdre, putting her on the spot.

"Do you have a cell phone on you?" asked Dierdre, silently annoyed at her husband.

"I sure do."

"Punch this in," she said, as she searched for Oyster Joe's address after tapping the contacts icon on her phone.

Smitty settled in at a chain hotel and began thinking things through. If Zamora turned out to be what he appeared to be then he was dealing with a dangerous man. A killer. On top of that, the old farmer lived on a private road absent neighbors.

Then he thought, 'I'll do a drive-by tonight, to the end of the road and back, acting like I'm lost. I'll drive real slow, check it out, and then drive right back to the hotel. No. Scratch that. If I were him, I'd be on guard at night. As would his dogs. I'll do it in the morning. That makes more sense. One wrong turn and you're on a dead end road. Not out of the ordinary. Much better than at nighttime. Nobody would think much of it during the daytime, and I'll be able to better see what I'm dealing with. That's what I'll do.'

Dan went to the gym. Finally. Dierdre waited five minutes before calling Oyster Joe on her business line. They'd met at a Chamber of Commerce event for business owners within a month or so after she and Dan moved to Shelton. She would call him now and again to get business advice. Joe was an experienced business owner who'd done good for himself and had a tendency to help others. For the most part, she kept her business dealings from her husband—not that he showed any interest.

Dierdre: Hi Joe, it's Dierdre. A weird thing happened today. A man came by our house looking for Rob Zamora. He said he was Rob's nephew. Dan opened his big mouth and mentioned that the only person around here who really knew Rob was you. Of course that prompted him to ask for your address and Dan turned and stared at me. I felt pressured and I gave it to him. I'm sorry.

Oyster Joe: Not a big deal. I haven't seen or heard from Rob since he sold the house and moved away. Funny thing, he never mentioned that he had a nephew. If he shows up, I'll have a chat with him. What's his name?

Dierdre: That's the thing, he didn't give us his name. And right now I'm feeling really, really stupid that I gave a stranger your address and didn't once ask him for his name. Jesus, that was dumb.

Oyster Joe: Forget about it. A lot of people know where I live. It's not a secret.

Dierdre: I hope to see you soon, Joe. And I'm sorry if I did anything wrong or put you in an awkward position.

Oyster Joe: You did nothing wrong, so don't go worrying about it. Take care, young lady.

Dierdre: Okay, Joe. Bye now.

At nine-fifteen in the morning he was driving down a private road. He felt an uneasiness in his stomach but attributed that to game-time nerves. The entire stretch of road extended a good quarter mile, with Oyster Joe's house sitting roughly two-thirds down the way on the right-hand side. Smitty's intuition intimated that no one was home.

It was a single story house—not big, not small. The old farmer lived on a healthy chunk of acreage that butted up against a heavily wooded area. It was fenced in on three sides. There was a big barn that dominated the land, with a shipping container positioned at the back of the property not far from the tree line. There were no cars in sight.

Smitty approached the dead end sign quicker than anticipated. He slowed his roll, maneuvered a three-point turn, and held steady while looking down the road from the opposite direction—from a different perspective. To his new left he saw a slice of curved silver extending out from behind the container. What's that? A trailer. How about that?

To his right was a sloping field that angled up sharply and ended at a dense tree line; an ideal location from which to view the farmer's compound. He could watch the old man from an elevated, hidden perch. He would be invisible.

Smitty drove away convinced that nobody was home, but someone—someone other than the owner—was living on the property. He could feel it. Bingo for the third time. Back to the hotel.

Fifteen minutes before first light, Smitty parked the rental car amid a group of trees. He had scouted out where to hike in the previous day. Feeling comfortable that the car was far enough off road and could not be seen by passing vehicles, he donned full camo gear and a backpack with necessary equipment stored inside. In his left hand was a flashlight, and holstered on his right thigh was a government issue semiautomatic pistol.

It took him every bit of ninety minutes to get to where he needed to be. And even though he was in decent gym shape, he was not in decent hiking shape when trudging across unfamiliar terrain—terrain sloped at sharp degrees of incline and decline—while also maneuvering on wet/dry/loose soil.

Hidden by a wall of thick greenery, he removed his backpack and coat. He was hot and sweaty, having built up a good lather. He unzipped one of the backpack's pockets and removed a canteen along with a hand towel.

After drinking almost all the water, he came to the quick conclusion that he should've packed a second canteen. Too late. He'd have to deal with it. Then he toweled off his face, neck and armpits.

After determining the best position to be in (comfortably concealed), he put a rifle scope up to his right eye and thoroughly surveilled Oyster Joe's property—from house to barn to container, from trailer to tree line to house. Nothing appeared different from the previous day, to include the lack of vehicles in the driveway. Was the Oyster farmer on vacation?

He stayed there well into the early afternoon—eight hours observing nothing but nature—before deciding to call it quits. Maybe he'd stop by Dan and Dierdre's the following day to see if they had an inkling as to the old man's whereabouts. He finished off what little water was left, barely a sip, and loaded up the backpack with all his gear before heading back to the car.

He was within a half mile of the rental car when he abruptly stopped in his tracks. He knew what he was looking at but was clearly baffled as to why it was there, as he silently asked himself, 'Did I miss this on the way in this morning?' For sure he wasn't returning on the exact same path he'd gone down earlier in the day, but he was close enough and this seemed too obvious to miss: a bright orange tractor parked in a small clearing with a shovel resting in its bucket.

Smitty sensed danger as the hair on the back of his neck stood on end, forcing him to slowly turn around as he put an unsteady hand on his gun.

He saw.

He heard.

He felt.

What he saw were two large dogs sitting at attention and eyeing him as if he was dinner.

What he heard was the release of—then the air being displaced by—a flying projectile.

What he felt was the bolt from a crossbow penetrating soft flesh and muscle at left oblique before exiting at lower right back, causing great internal organ damage and slicing through and through at an angle in sync with the shooter's intentions. He had five minutes to live, tops.

The next thing Smitty realized was that an old man was crouching over him—removing his backpack and gun as if undressing a sleeping child. He said something in another language that sounded a lot like German.

With his face resting on forest floor, Smitty could see both dogs still sitting there, just sitting there. They hadn't moved. Why was that?

He heard the old man ask him a question in English that he couldn't quite make out. 'Must be bilingual,' he thought. But the only two words Smitty could muster were "Help" and "me," and those were wasted words at this point in the game because help wasn't coming, and it wasn't being offered.

Smitty was young and expendable. And as he took his final breath, he still hadn't figured that out.

Oyster Joe hiked out with Smitty's backpack. The dogs stayed put. He'd be back to finish the job.

There was a man leaning against Smitty's rental car patiently waiting for the oyster farmer. Joe handed him the backpack, and said, "The car keys and the phone are in the front pouch."

The man took hold of the backpack, removed the keys, unlocked the rental car and got inside. After starting the engine, he powered down the window, and said, "Bill said to say thanks. Said you shouldn't have any more problems."

Joe stood there for a brief moment, before saying, "Well, you tell that old-timer I said he's more than welcome. And, I hope he's right about there being no more problems."

As the man drove off, Oyster Joe walked back into the woods.

Fifty-three

There they sat. Same four. Same place. New problem.

The leader, Number One, spoke first: He's missing. His rental car turned up in Seattle. There were no keys inside and it was completely wiped clean. No prints. He never checked out of the hotel in Shelton, and he left behind a change of clothes and a shave kit. Then I got this in the mail (holding up Smitty's cell phone). At my fucking house. Can you believe that? The only thing on it is a single text message.

Number Two: I received his Glock 19 in the mail. Also sent to my home address.

Number Three: I received the full clip belonging to that gun.

Number Four (the lone dissenter from their previous meeting): And what did the text message say?

Number One: Three words, all caps, with a period after each word. LET. IT. GO.

Three of the four sat silent as Number Three mumbled unintelligible words drenched in fear.

Number One to Number Four: What did you get in the mail?

Number Four: Funny you should ask. I received a large padded envelope. Inside were the keys to his rental car and a brochure for an Airstream trailer.

They all pondered the meaning of the brochure.

Finally, Number One spoke: Are we all in agreement that we should let it go?

Four men answered identically.

The unanimous decision won out.

Fifty-four

They met at the airport, flying in from different locales—each living in a big city and enjoying the change. It had been quite a while since they'd been together. But catching up wasn't necessary because they spoke daily on the phone.

Coming home can be an interesting venture. Rarely does it seem like it used to be, at least not when compared to a decade past. An adult's perspective about a childhood lived is usually overhyped or undersold, and at times completely omitted. Memories. Real or imagined. Are they really worth it?

They were there for their mother. A rare ask. They quickly agreed to meet after hearing an earnestness seep from her voice. And here they were, mother and daughters—their father out of town attending a seminar. She hadn't told them what it was about, not entirely, and avoided the subject altogether while they dined.

After dinner they moved to the living room. Once the twins were settled in, she went to her bedroom and, shortly thereafter, returned with two brown packages. She handed over a package to each daughter.

They both asked, "What's this?"

"A gift from your late uncle," replied Maria. Then, suddenly realizing they had two dead uncles, she revised her reply. "From Uncle Blue, and no need opening either one."

Now they were really confused. "Why wouldn't we open our gifts?"

"Because he left you two million dollars each. And I don't want money flying around my living room like it's confetti being tossed about at a drunken sorority party. I'm your mother, and let's not forget that I know you two better than you know yourselves."

"Are you serious?" they asked.

"About the money or the drunken sorority parties?" asked Maria.

"About the money, Mom."

"Oh, that. Yeah, I'm very serious. Now let's discuss what to do with it. But only if you want to keep it," Maria replied sarcastically.

They discussed money and death well into the evening.

Maria and the girls walked toward the forest; her brother's urn held tight to her breast. The twins were barefoot, each in a sundress and ready to take Uncle Blue back to that special place.

It had to have been a combination of the girls and nature, their unwavering love plus the trees and coastal fog. That's what stood out in her mind. That's what would always stand out in her mind when she went back to that place: earthy smells, salt-splashed air, love, tranquility.

It was like the twins and the trees and the fog were communicating without words. And she was one hundred percent sober. She wasn't always sober. But rarely was she excessively impaired, with cannabis being her substance of choice. Still, it was like a psychedelic experience without drugs. If that's possible. It was, because from that day forward she'd look back on that experience for spiritual comfort and joy.

They meandered for a good half hour deep into the woods, at last standing before an ancient, majestic redwood. The enormity and height of this erect sentinel was visually overwhelming, stunning. The twins had no problem finding it. Throughout their lives they'd returned to this sacred place often enough, keeping it a secret as if gifted from a higher source.

In her brief wanderings Maria had never witnessed such a tree, at least not in person. And yet there it was in her own backyard. Knowing that she was in the presence of royalty, she hesitantly reached out and touched it, her hand slowly tracing downward, ever respectful. Its trunk's bark was deeply etched; over-pronounced braille emanating a story for those willing to listen.

Together they sat on the padded forest floor facing the tree, a twin at each side. The fog moved in—much, much thicker—encasing them in a misty-white blanket. Maria was suddenly overcome by an unexplained deep emotional love and began to weep, as did the twins. All at once they looked up at the giant redwood, its trunk expanding in then out, breathing, shuttering at times, as they all wept in unison.

An understanding. Everyone. Everything. Connected.

Then sleep.

Upon awakening, Maria opened the urn and poured Uncle Blue's ashes into cupped hands. They spread his ashes at trunk's edge—three different spots where if connected by straight lines formed a triangle. They pressed human dust into accepting soil. When done, they held hands and stood in silence.

At last, homeward bound.

Fifty-five

False status doesn't bring wisdom, and a single ideology shouldn't be the only blueprint followed. Those were some of the words he spoke as he sat on the hood of a rental car, his friend's backside, a shabby house, and nature his entire audience. They discussed quite a few things that day in the Pacific Northwest—Johnny using words, Rob using nonverbal gestures and silence. And while Johnny Blue unveiled his grand plan, his comrade listened intently.

As the meeting wound down, they made a pact of finality. They definitely did that. A suicide of friends. One wanting to make a lasting statement, the other ready to exit the world.

He lived and he died. And as a prearranged death approached, he knew that his words had swayed others to kill and to be killed. So at a fraction of a second before death, as he looked out over a throng of people, he understood completely that what separated him from the others—those wielding power and exerting selfish influence—was that he did it for the people and the betterment of society and not to hold on to power or influence or wealth.

He died knowing exactly what he was, for regrets he did not have. Regrets were a waste of time, unless, of course, they're tied to lies, apathy, enduring rationalizations and lifelong excuses. Regrets are for the many false advertisers—unable to comprehend that there are no do-overs even as they approach final exhale.

You do what you do.

You own it.

And you live with it.

Acknowledgements

Many thanks to A.L. Cameron for her editing skills, keen observations, intelligent suggestions and unwavering patience.

Also, much gratitude to A.K. for her continued insight and honest communication.

And finally, a special thanks to M.E. (Montanha) for an educated history on Brazilian Jiu-jitsu, and the philosophical coffeehouse conversations that challenge my thinking.

Made in the USA
Columbia, SC
22 December 2019

85647428R00114